NA
G
EMERALD HILL

This easy-to-read novel is about six girls, five charming Singaporean misses and one lovable Japanese madam. Their exciting adventures are unravelled against the beautiful and romantic, yet at times dangerous, surroundings of war-time Emerald Hill where the Singapore girls lived together in a hostel.

NAN-MEI-SU or the House of Southern Beauties was a comfort house set up by the Japanese Army in Cairnhill. The writer GOH SIN TUB lived nearby in Emerald Hill then and in writing this work of fiction, he has drawn from his recollections of actual events during the Japanese Occupation– and of the Nan-mei-su girls. From facts he weaves fascinating fiction about their loves, their brushes with the notorious Japanese Kempeitai, their clashes with the *samsengs* (gangsters).

A Singapore creative writer of recognised standing, Goh has now produced for Singaporeans our country's first historical novel covering this tumultous time in our past, set in a locale which has become the foremost nostalgic heritage neighbourhood in Singapore. With his flair for humour and the dramatic and his understanding of human nature, Goh's latest work will no doubt be enjoyed by Singaporeans (and others too) in search of good, entertaining Singapore literature.

WRITING IN ASIA SERIES

THE NAN-MEI-SU GIRLS OF EMERALD HILL

Goh Sin Tub

HEINEMANN ASIA

Singapore

Published by
**Heinemann Asia, a Division of
Octopus Publishing Asia Pte Ltd**
37 Jalan Pemimpin #07-04, Block B
Union Industrial Building
Singapore 2057

OXFORD   LONDON   EDINBURGH   MELBOURNE   SYDNEY
AUCKLAND   MADRID   ATHENS   IBADAN   NAIROBI
GABORONE   HARARE   KINGSTON   PORTSMOUTH (NH)

ISBN 9971-64-199-2

© Goh Sin Tub 1989
First published 1989
Reprinted 1989

Cover photo taken at Bibi's Theatre Pub, Peranakan Place.

Typeset by Graphics Services Pte. Ltd.
Printed by Denko Press Pte. Ltd.

Contents

Contents

CHAPTER ONE

Doris

Sue Ann sat in her parked BMW staring at the house in quiet Emerald Hill. She had come in from Australia. All the way to view that house — and the restored neighbourhood. Emerald Hill was now a treasured national heritage. The Singapore Government had gazetted the houses on the Hill for preservation. It had improved the environment. The road was beautifully tiled, landscaping added freshness to it, traffic was now sparse due to access control. The houses advertised for sale were now highly priced and the Hill was becoming exclusive.

Sue Ann knew that house well. Once upon a time. The exterior had not changed much since those days ("Goodness! more than thirty years ago!") when she lived there with Doris. And Sleepy and Lily and the rest. Yes, and dear May too, now dead and gone.

That was during the Japanese Occupation. There, in that house the girls were thrown together. And they became a family.

Now this house, their old home, was up for sale. Yes, soon it would belong to her, Sue Ann, the girl who first came here as a frightened teenage girl from a poor family.

She was there to meet Mr Ramasamy, the real estate agent who advertised the property for sale. She was early — deliberately. She wanted to look around a bit first, savour the old surroundings, wallow a bit in nostalgia.

The current owner of the house was probably some respectable Singaporean professional/businessman/civil servant with his obedient stopped-at-two-now-trying-hard-to-go-on-to-three family.

Sue Ann smiled. It was hard to think of this house as the one-time home of those girls of Emerald Hill, the girls of Nan-mei-su.

But the memories came back easily enough to her.

The house was not exactly their home, it was more their hostel, a convenient nearby place for the girls to sleep in at night or during the day whenever off-duty from their hard work as waitresses at that club. That notorious comfort house at nearby Cairnhill Road for Japanese officers and soldiers. Nan-mei-su or the House of Southern Beauties.

They themselves were not the official Beauties. Others were. Geishas from Japan and others. They were merely the servers of sustenance and the deliverers of drinks, not the providers of passionate pleasures, though from time to time a few of them would be invited or might themselves ask to transfer over.

Sue Ann recalled her first arrival at this Emerald Hill hostel which was to be for her a happier home than what she came from. Doris, bigger than her and thoroughly motherly, although not much older than Sue Ann's seventeen years, brought her over from Nan-mei-su. Sue Ann had been brought to the club by her step-mother who had scolded her *"Gong cha boh!* (stupid girl!), go right in and ask for that waitress job.

"Remember! they tell you, you do! Anything, understand? Don't care what, just do! Don't get sacked, understand? We need the money, understand?" Those were her step-mother's loving last words as she abandoned her at the front gate of the club before the sentry's hut.

She had gone up to the Japanese sentry, calm outside but shivering inside. She bowed deeply before that almighty (a full ninety-degree obeisance, which was the tribute paid, before the Japanese invaders came, to few other than the dead in their coffins). She spoke the few words she had rehearsed in broken Nippongo and to her relief gained instant admission to the row of buildings barbed-wired off to form the Nan-mei-su camp.

She met the Japanese manageress. She was a surprisingly friendly lady. In her early thirties, plump, fair and smooth-skinned, firm yet gentle, more like a convent mother-superior than a comfort-house madam.

She held Sue Ann's hands and her eyes searched deep but not unfriendly beneath the young girl's brave front and somehow the latter knew at once there would be sympathy and care from this stranger, more than she received at home.

"Call me Mama-san, *neh!* Everybody calls me Mama-san," she told Sue Ann.

Mama-san then called out for Doris, who seemed to

be her unofficial assistant for just about everything. Doris took over and brought Sue Ann to Emerald Hill.

"Sue Ann? Nice name! OK, just get one thing straight. Here in this house I am the boss. Mama-san put me in charge, OK? Everything I say goes. Everything! Keep the rules and you'll be happy staying here. First rule: This place is for us only. Nobody else allowed in here, no boyfriends, no customers from the club, no relatives or friends. Nobody except we Nan-mei-su waitresses. This is our own place. Remember!"

Doris left no room for any doubt. But still that rule was to be broken a few times. Even by Doris herself.

"Suppose soldiers follow us home? Suppose they want to come in?" Sue Ann asked timidly.

"What for, you worry? They know, lah! They have to keep their fun to inside the club. That's the rule for them. The hostesses serve them there... Remember, our jobs are not that kind! We are waitresses, nothing more, understand? Anybody wants to be hostess, OK, fine! Just ask Mama-san for transfer. She'll arrange. First, medical test and security check, then transfer."

"Suppose soldiers just don't care, just want to come in? You know, drunk.. "

"Easy! Just phone Kempeitai, you know, MP's. They'll come and *gasak* (wallop) them," May, who had come over, chipped in with a laugh: "Just say magic word 'Kempeitai', and like magic, they *chabok* (scoot off) straightaway like lightning, man! Where got need to phone some more?"

May, always as plain-speaking as she was plain-looking, was to become Sue Ann's close friend. Her straight hair, her dark complexion (so dark that Sue Ann's own brownness looked fair beside hers), and her skinny frame did nothing for her. Yet she managed to grow on you, become attractive in her own way; once you started talking with her, her no-nonsense goodness and disarming frankness will warm your heart. Dear May, a jewel of a friend... dead and gone. And the rest of the girls gone too... lost into the wide world as they scrambled out of that unreal world of the Occupation. Scattered in their panic to get away.

Sue Ann smiled as she thought of Doris. She was the big sister she never had until she joined Nan-mei-su. Now, that was certainly one lady who knew how to handle people. Nobody, but nobody, tangled with Doris. She could be rough and tough as they came. And yet she had always an uncanny understanding of people and she knew just when to soften and give way.

Made in the image and likeness of Mama-san, but less jumbo-sized than the Japanese lady, Doris was a natural-born leader. And she would have been our head of household even if she did not have that authority officially conferred on her. Sue Ann smiled with fondness in her heart as she recalled that pillar of strength.

She ordered us around but she cared for us, really cared as she proved on many occasions. So the girls might grumble or plead or throw a tantrum but in the end they would always obey her.

Where was she now? Was she still alive? Dear big-sister Doris! Always in command, always capable, ready to deal with any situation...

Such as that first encounter with the gangsters of the neighbourhood! Sue Ann's first of several brushes with the underworld, and her first experience of Doris in action, how strong and cool and yet shrewd and understanding she could be.

One night when Lily came home to the hostel, three tough-looking characters followed her up the Hill and insisted on coming into the front hall. Lily, who was a natural flirt with her coquettish eyes and wiggling walk, did not put up much of a resistance. Later on she claimed they pushed their way in before she could close the door.

But as it turned out they had business rather than pleasure in mind though, from the way one of them ogled Lily, they would not be averse to pleasure once their business was done and out of the way.

They told Lily they wanted to talk to the person in charge. Doris heard unfamiliar voices inside the house and came downstairs at once. Sue Ann followed her. The other girls hung back, peeping from the inner hall which served as their dining room.

"We are here to help you. We have decided we'll look after you girls," said their leader who introduced himself as Ah Lek. He was a soft-voiced slim young man with steely eyes and a determined jaw. He spoke slowly and with care.

"What you mean, look after us?" Sue Ann asked suspiciously but as she spoke out of turn she received a clear shut-up-let-me-do-the-talking glare from Doris.

"You stop talking rubbish! Just say what you want." Doris showed she remained in control. She gained a quick glance of respect from Ah Lek.

"Well, you know, it's the same everywhere. In your kind of work you girls need protection. And that's what we can give you. We're organised. We know how to persuade people to do things. Or not to do things. It won't cost you much. We're not greedy. We only want for our expenses... say, $60 a month. That's cheap, only five or six dollars each from the 10 or 12 of you in this house. That's reasonable, isn't it? Think of the peace of mind you get!"

"Sorry! We're not paying," Doris said bluntly.

"Not paying?" Ah Lek repeated softly, eyes closed and silent for an electrifying minute.

One of his henchmen let out an animal snort. The other sucked in his breath and started clenching his fists and tensing his ample biceps, which diversion sent thrills of fright and what-nots down the spine of Sue Ann who had a ring-side seat right next to this muscular display. The two men looked ready to explode.

Ah Lek stopped them with a twitch of his eyebrow.

Doris and Ah Lek remained silent, each sizing the other up, trying to read each other's minds. That exchange of chemistry started off something which the others were not aware of till much later.

"Maybe you don't understand. This is our place. Everybody doing business here pays us, each a little bit. Two or three dollars from the hawkers, $20 from the coffee-shop, $30 from the provision-shop... Everyone feeds us a little," Ah Lek explained patiently.

"Why, we're like beggars, man! We live on people's charity," Ah Lek let out a dry laugh, which his assistants immediately echoed. They liked the joke.

He continued on an even tone: "On our part we keep the peace. We guarantee you no one gets bullied. No other gang comes to *kachau* (bother) you. We give you good service... "

Doris remained silent but her eyes though determined showed no hostility, indeed there was now understanding.

"What will others say if we let you go without paying?" Ah Lek asked.

"They won't say anything. You see, we're not doing business. We're only waitresses. Not hostesses, as many people think. We're wage-earners not *towkays* ... We don't earn anything, only our salaries, you know."

"Huh! We know what you are," Ah Lek's right-hand man leered.

"Shut up, Ah Sai!" the gangster silenced his man with a sudden snarl. Then a quick switch to a smile for Doris and a soft last word:

"Think about it for a day or two. Our protection is so cheap. In these times everyone needs protection. You think the Japs will look after you? They only look after their own. And the police are useless, they can't do much... What if some unreasonable gang comes and really squeezes all of you? Think about that... "

"You also think about what I said. You've made a mistake with us. We are only wage-earners, and we don't earn much," Doris replied cool as ice-kachang.

Ah Lek stood there motionless. Doris studied him intently. Perhaps she saw beneath his tough exterior, perhaps even at that first encounter she read more than the others could in the dark depths of those unblinking eyes. She felt his dilemma, understood his hesitation, knew that in a moment he would have to react brutally as expected of him by his lieutenants. Unless she could provide a reason for him to soften. Perhaps this was the unspoken message as he looked steadily into her eyes.

She changed her tone suddenly.

She pleaded. She even managed a whine in her voice. The other girls couldn't believe their ears. Sue Ann was close enough to see that some signal had been transmitted but even she could not understand Doris's move till viewed in retrospect later.

"Please pity us. You know, we're only poor working girls! Why be so tough on us? We don't earn much at all, not like those hostesses! Please, I ask you!"

That made the difference.

Ah Lek smiled, understanding in his eyes and a hint of gratitude as well. He said nothing more. Just got up and left.

And that was the last the girls heard of that extortion bid.

It was not the last they heard or saw of Ah Lek. They saw him around the place, doing his "policing", collecting his dues from others, occasionally even greeting the girls as they walked by, especially Doris with whom he always tried to strike up a friendly conversation.

Then one day the girls heard the news.

Mama-san told them that the Kempeitai had picked up one Ah Lek, a suspected gangster whom they believed to be connected with some saboteurs as well. They were looking for witnesses who could give information on the man's activities, his associates, etc.

In the privacy of their house, Doris warned the girls to say nothing.

"He let us off, so we let him off too!" Doris laid down their stand.

And for the benefit of any who might be wavering, Doris added: "The Kempeitai will use those who cooperate with them. They'll use you again and again. They'll make you do more spying for them and trapping people. You'll get in deeper and deeper. Then you can't get out... And Ah Sai and the others, you think they won't be watching — and waiting to get you?"

The girls were convinced, their heads nodding obediently. And after all, why not? Ah Lek had now taken on the glow of a Resistance helper.

Indeed some of the girls even shed tears for Ah Lek. He was handsome in his rough-cut way, he was friendly for a dangerous fellow, now he was elevated to the status of a secret hero, and furthermore the situation looked hopeless for him — all perfect ingredients for romantic swooning.

The Kempeitai might be asking around for witnesses, but everyone knew they did not really need any. Sooner or later, guilty or otherwise, they wrapped up their cases with confessions extracted through the diabolical devices in the notorious torture chambers of their HQ in the converted former YMCA building in Stamford Road.

But there was to be more drama to the Ah Lek episode.

"Have you girls heard the latest news about Ah Lek?" Mama-san asked the girls one morning not many days later.

They had not. After all how many of them had contacts with the Kempeitai like Mama-san's. Her beau was a full Colonel who functioned as some kind of Kempeitai liaison.

"He confessed?" May, realistic and direct, jumped to the obvious dreaded conclusion.

"Died under torture?" Lily ventured hopefully with the occasional frivolous sadism of the very young, getting a dirty look from Doris for her pains.

"No," Mama-san revealed. "He escaped!"

"He escaped from the Kempeitai?" The girls just couldn't believe it. Few people ever escaped from the Kempeitai.

"What a guy!" Doris let out involuntarily. Which made Mama-san look at her curiously.

"They're hunting for him. They'll catch him sure! Where can he go? Where can he hide? Only a fool will dare to hide him. And when they find him that's the end of him. They'll chop off his head!" Mama-san said deliberately, studying Doris casually from the sides of her eyes.

But Doris was now in full control. She even managed a cool: "Of course!"

"And maybe they'll hang his head outside the YMCA, as they did last time with those looters!" Lily added hopefully. This time all the girls, and even Mama-san, looked daggers at her.

Then a series of puzzling things soon began to happen about Doris.

On Sunday nights Doris would go home to her house not far off in River Valley Road where she stayed with her mother and auntie, both in their sixties. It was really an illegal shed adjoining a row of ancient shophouses so neglected some had plants and small trees growing from their walls and roofs. The place was tiny but sufficient for their shelter, especially with Doris away most of the time.

On Sunday night Doris went home which was usual, but the next morning she was late reporting at Nan-mei-su, which was not usual. She told Mama-san her mother was not well and she had to attend to her.

Then Doris started going home every other night, leaving May in charge of the Emerald Hill hostel. Same reason: Mother's ill health.

Mama-san offered to arrange for medical treatment, but Doris quickly turned her down. "It's old age, that's all. Besides, she only goes for Chinese medicine."

However she did accept some *Wakamoto* (vitamin) pills from Mama-san.

The girls wanted to pay the old lady a visit, but Doris vetoed the idea. "She don't like people to come. She gets grumpy like hell — and gets worse!"

Doris also began to bring home a lot more food than before. By custom the girls were allowed to take home the club's left-over food but only for their own family's consumption.

"Mother's so sick, can't cook, you know."

"She seems to eat more!" Lily observed. "You never take home so much before." This was meant to be a joke but Doris was flustered and annoyed, which was quite unlike her.

Indeed Doris seemed generally more edgy and also more preoccupied. Something was definitely bothering her, perhaps her mother's illness was more serious than Doris wished to let on.

Then one day May, looking worried, pulled Sue Ann aside and whispered to her, "You know what? Guess who I bumped into at the market?.. Doris's mother! One hundred percent fit, man! Not sick kind lah! I can see, what? Walking about, buying things. But, I say, she was so nervous! Dropped her basket when I touched her arm! Then she recognized me but still she just stood there, mouth open like ready to catch flies ... And you know what she buying? Second-hand clothes, men's clothes! Why? They got no men in their house? I tell you, that Doris is hiding something..."

"Or someone?" Sue Ann spoke the unthinkable. Softly but loud enough.

Both girls gasped at the thought! The risk Doris was taking! They decided to ask her about it the moment

they could get her alone without the other girls
around.

"Doris, we know, man! Don't try to bluff. You're
hiding that fellow Ah Lek at your house, right?"

May's question popped out in her usual blunt
manner. More like a statement of fact defying denial.
She and Sue Ann had managed to get Doris alone at
last, but only as Doris was already homeward-bound
on her walk down Emerald Hill. The two girls walked
down with her.

Doris looked at her two friends, read the anxiety in
their eyes, made an intuitive decision and bit back the
"no!" already at the tip of her tongue.

She nodded more with her eyes than her head.

The Emerald Hill full moon bathed the three of
them in ghostly light as they walked down past the
rows of peacefully sleeping houses. Sue Ann
remembered it all felt so much of the unreal world,
Doris getting involved in such a dangerous thing.
Harbouring a fugitive from the Kempeitai!

Sue Ann recalled she walked with her friends in the
moonlight like she was in a dream. She half-expected
to wake up from it any moment. For a second she felt
a cowardly impulse to run away. But that did not last;
she had learnt from her brief childhood that running
away didn't work — sooner or later all situations had
to be faced. She pictured Ah Lek being thrashed by
the Kempeitai, and she thought of her own thrashings
from her step-mother. Her heart went out to him.

She took Doris's ever-warm hand. She said simply,
"Don't worry, Doris. I'll help you."

The two girls looked into each other's eyes. They

merged in a hug of love.

May's eyes shuttled between the two crazy girls.
These two were supposed to be her best friends in the
world! Yet they were both letting her down so badly,
behaving so stupidly in these dangerous times. She
wanted to argue with them, shake them by their
shoulders, bring them to their senses, get them to give
up their crazy idea of helping the man, surrender him
to the Kempeitai...

But something strange came over her — the magic
of Emerald Hill moonlight, spell of lunacy, absolute
giddy-headedness, a kind of high. She watched in
jealous fascination Sue Ann's surrender of soul to
Doris, watched the beauty of the response as the two
girls left her and the rest of the world, held hands and
embraced in a love which excluded everything and
everyone else, made everything else unimportant.

May had to be part of that...

May said nothing. She had found the love, but not
the words. Words were superfluous anyway. She
joined in.

The three friends stood there, locked in their
embrace, happy, childishly happy, though without any
solution to their problem.

A couple of elderly residents walked past them,
looked at them with distaste, turned their scandalized
eyes away.

"Nan-mei-su girls! No shame! *Mabok sahaja!* (Drunk
only!) And doing what funny things, who knows?
Right out here in our streets, too!" the old lady
muttered loudly.

The girls heard her but they did not care. They had
heard worse things about themselves, the Nan-mei-su
girls. Let people say what they want, let them label

you as they like, you can't stop them anyway. It's what you do and what's in your heart that really matters.

Sue Ann was sure all the girls at their hostel would help, they were all sympathetic to Ah Lek, and they would listen to Doris.

All, that is except Lily. Sue Ann was not sure about Lily. Doris agreed with Sue Ann. But May, who knew Lily longer, said she was OK, she could be persuaded, she could be arm-twisted.

The three girls agreed it was too dangerous for Ah Lek to continue to hide in Doris's place. It was too small and there were too many people living around them, some even working for the Japanese government departments.

Ah Lek's Resistance friends had been in touch with Doris. They just needed a few more days to finalise arrangements, then they would come in a car and take Ah Lek away. Then by boat to the deserted beaches and the jungles of Malaya.

Sue Ann and May urged that Ah Lek should be moved to their hostel. Doris was not keen at first. It would be too risky for the girls. But in the end, out of sheer desperation she had to agree. For she received information that the Japanese were about to launch a house-to-house search in her neighbourhood any moment now!

"How did you find out that, Doris? The house-to-house search?" May was curious.

"Mama-san told me."

"She told you? Just like that?"

"Yes, she just came out with it. I wonder why... Could have been just chit-chat. Or else what?"

"Yes, what?" There was a contradiction of both hope and fear in May's voice, both of which her two companions understood.

"Mama-san's trying to save you, Doris," Sue Ann voiced their hope. "She's helping us, she's on our side."

"She knows! Sure she knows you're hiding him. At least she suspects... Maybe she will report you? Sooner or later," May spoke out their fear.

"Better get him out of your place straightaway," she concluded.

"The soldiers won't search our hostel," Sue Ann pointed out. "They've always been told, our house is out-of-bounds to them."

"Besides, we are the Nan-mei-su girls, aren't we? The friends of the Japanese soldiers?" she added with a smile.

Now that the move was agreed, the problem was how to put it to the girls. More specifically, how to win over Lily.

The three girls decided they had to put it across straight — no time for any other way. Call in all the girls after work, which would be around midnight, put the proposal to everyone and wait for their reaction. Especially Lily's. And play it by ear from there.

You can imagine the open-mouthed reaction of the Nan-mei-su girls. When the ooh's and aah's had died down and the impact of the proposal (and its dangers) had sunk in, there was a moment of silence. It was also a moment of test. For the loyalty which Doris commanded from these girls. She had bossed over them and even punished some but she had always loved them as her own family and they knew it. They always came to her with their problems, even Lily. They could always count on her for help.

As Sue Ann had anticipated, the girls came out in full support. Even Lily, to the surprise (and relieved shame) of the three girls who had doubted her. True, there was a bit of hesitation on everyone's part at the start, as the enormity of what they would be doing sunk in.

Then one of the girls asked Doris:

"Sorry, Doris, first I must ask you a personal question. Please tell me, is Ah Lek somebody special to you? Is he your... Well, you know what I mean..."

For a split second Doris remained silent.

Then she said, "The answer is ... yes!"

Sue Ann looked at her friend. Was Doris telling the truth, the whole truth, and nothing but...? Sue Ann felt it was more likely Doris herself did not know the real answer; at that point she was just helping Ah Lek to gain sanctuary. Doris had never mentioned to May or herself that there was anything between herself and Ah Lek.

The only other person who seemed unsure of Doris's confession was Lily. Her sharp eyes must have caught the momentary hesitation for she quickly chipped in: "Ah Lek's mine if Doris is not claiming him!"

The girls ignored her.

Doris's answer was enough for them. They no longer held back. Yes, they would help to hide Ah Lek till his friends could organise his disappearance.

Ah Lek's friends managed his clandestine arrival at

Emerald Hill. His second coming was not as macho (but then also not as unwelcome) as his first arrival. Indeed, the very opposite.

He came disguised as a Nan-mei-su girl and with his slim figure he looked the role.

The girls were assembled inside, waiting for him. Once the doors were closed they exploded into giggles and guffaws. To which he responded with a mock show of girlish shyness and much wiggling of his skirted bottom to the delight of everyone. The girls then, one and all, hugged him and made it clear to him he was welcome.

Not least of all, Lily who gave him a thoroughly wet kiss with more than a hint of linger as she held him tight in her clinger of an embrace that was only forcibly disengaged by the combined power of other impatient loving arms and lips in the queue.

Last but not least in the kissing line was Doris. She sensed she was on centre stage. She started off with, as was expected of her, a more-than-sisterly embrace, which heated up to passionate proportions as he got over his initial surprise and responded with ardour. And then she too began to enter into the spirit of the thing.

Sue Ann wondered if Doris had started it off as a show, that is, before it gained a life of its own. No such doubt sullied the pure voyeuristic pleasure of the other girls who gawked for an indecent while, then burst out into applause punctured by squeals of vicarious ecstasy. When Doris came out of that clinch, her eyes looked dazed. And to Sue Ann, confused. But pleasurably confused.

May looked sweet in her frank happiness for her friend.

Lily looked sour.

Back at Nan-mei-su, Mama-san went about looking so worried that Doris had to speak up.

"If you're worried for me, Mama-san, it's OK now. I've solved my problem at home." Doris's eyes tried to say more than her lips dared to voice, more than what Mama-san's Japanese ears should hear.

Mama-san's eyes rested for a second on her assistant. For a moment she remained silent. Then she said, "I don't know what your problem was, and I don't want to know. But I'm glad it's over. Now we can get back to worrying about our work, *neh*?"

That evening the Kempeitai searched Doris's home. They found nothing. They were checking the entire neighbourhood. Some informer could have spotted Ah Lek in that crowded cluster of old houses. The Kempeitai kicked around a little, slapped around a bit, shouted at everybody within range, but left without any arrests.

"I suppose they'll be giving up the search?" Doris asked Mama-san innocently when Mama-san told her about the unsuccessful hunt which she had heard about from her Colonel.

"No," Mama-san replied looking anxiously into Doris's eyes. "They believe he's still around here somewhere. They'll widen their search. House-to-house... I hope none of our girls are so foolish, I hope none of them are hiding the man at home! The Kempeitai are very angry, they'll show no mercy to anyone hiding him!"

"None of our girls are doing that, hiding the man at their own homes, I'm sure of that, Mama-san."

"How can you be so sure?"

Doris left the question unanswered. Perhaps she should have answered her. But how could she?

A single man staying in a hostel of fifteen healthy admiring young girls is a situation pregnant with possibilities. But the circumstances protected Ah Lek from close encounters of the lewd kind. The period of stay was only a short few days, the hostel was too crowded, but most of all he was the boss lady's boy-friend.

The only one undeterred was Lily.

She slipped off from duty one afternoon telling one of the girls she couldn't stand it, she had to go off, she was suffering from an awful bout of diarrhoea.

And so it came to pass that she was home at Emerald Hill with Ah Lek. Alone.

What happened that afternoon nobody knew for sure.

They say that hell has no fury like a woman scorned.

When the girls came back that night they found a furious Lily, for some reason angry and emotional, although she seemed fully recovered from her stomach upset.

"What's the matter, Lily?" Sue Ann asked.

"It's all this bloody tension, all this risk we're taking... And for who? For a useless *samseng* (gangster) chief! Why, the bastard even tried to squeeze us for money before! Why should we risk ourselves for him!" Lily burst out with sudden spite and venom.

"What happened, Lily?" May asked pointedly, a mockingly innocent look in her eyes.

"What happened? What do you mean, what happened? Nothing, that's what. Nothing!"

Her frustration degenerated to malignancy as she realised she had said it all. And got no sympathy from anyone.

Doris went over to talk with Ah Lek who had of course heard everything, the house being small. They were close that evening.

Lily went out of the house in a huff.

May did not like it at all.

"You know, that Lily, she does crazy things when she's crazy. Like one time she got so mad with her boyfriend, you know what she did? She got some gangsters to beat him up..." May shared her uneasiness with Sue Ann.

The two decided to have a frank talk with Lily when she came back.

They never had the chance. Events moved too fast for them.

Doris was summoned to Mama-san's office the moment she stepped into Nan-mei-su early the next morning.

"Doris," she closed the door and began quietly and deliberately. "Don't I deserve your trust? Have we not become good friends?"

"Yes, but you are — "

"Japanese?"

"Yes. And because you are also my friend, some things I just cannot tell you."

"Like about your boyfriend Ah Lek hiding in Emerald Hill?"

Doris looked at Mama-san — distress, anxiety, panic,

mixed emotions in her eyes. Then she saw that Mama-san was just as worried. She felt her motherly concern. Her tears flowed out in relief and tacit confession. Mama-san took her child into her comforting arms.

After a while, Doris asked, "How did you know?"

"I suspected it after our last talk. But last night Lily came. She told me everything. She was crying, upset and confused like a child. She also pleaded with me to let her become a geisha, a Nan-mei-su hostess. I agreed but just to calm her down. I told her, not to say anything to anybody else and to leave everything to me. She's now gone to stay with one of the hostesses for a while..."

"She's a swine — " Doris began.

"Don't be too hard on her," Mama-san interrupted. "She still cares for all of you, her friends. She told me many times to make sure the girls don't get into trouble. She said to tell the Kempeitai that Ah Lek forced his way in and is terrorizing the girls."

Doris was not impressed but reverted to the urgent question: "What to do now?"

"I have to report to the Kempeitai. You know that. But I'll delay. I'll think of some excuse. You get back now and get Ah Lek's friends to move him out straightaway. And tell the girls to stick to Lily's story when the Kempeitai come — Ah Lek forced his way in and terrorized all of you."

Doris rushed back. Sue Ann and May helped her to reassure the girls and steady their nerves. Doris handled Ah Lek's exit. Fortunately, his friends were ready to spirit him out of the country.

Sue Ann remembered the frantic yet tender farewell between the lovers. They held hands. They embraced. They kissed.

Ah Lek, a Buddhist, said, "If we don't meet again in this life, I will seek you in my reincarnation."

Doris, to whom Sue Ann had talked about the compassionate God she learnt about in her Convent school, said, "No! God is good, He will bring us together again."

Sue Ann would recall that night often. How could she forget such a night?

The girls of Nan-mei-su put on an academy award performance. Once Ah Lek was safely away with the few hours' headstart he needed, the girls gave the all-clear signal to the waiting Mama-san. While she summoned her Colonel friend on the phone with all the excitement she could muster, the girls spoke hysterically to the Kempeitai using the emergency phone number which they had been given, screaming blue murder.

The Kempeitai came. They questioned the girls. Actually only Doris and May, since those two were the only ones who spoke Nippongo well enough. They corroborated each other's stories while the other girls just did a lot of nodding and miming of an imaginary gangster with a gun ordering them around.

That evening the rest of Emerald Hill was ransacked from top to bottom and not a few residents were bashed about. But all the Kempeitai found was one miserable deaf old man trying to listen to BBC news (he did not even hear the Kempeitai coming) and one black marketeer with illegal hoards of British currency and Japanese cigarettes.

Of Ah Lek there was not a trace.

After that, the girls heard through Mama-san's

reliable sources that he had escaped the Kempeitai's clutches and disappeared into the comparative safety of the jungle.

CHAPTER TWO

Sue Ann and Momo

S ue Ann got out of her car. She needed to stretch her legs and she wanted to take a look around. The neighbourhood still looked familiar, like when she and the other Nan-mei-su girls lived here. And yet it was different.

Yes, the place still looked traditional Emerald Hill, perhaps in a way more so than ever, what with the URA going great guns in their enthusiastic interpretation of the old and quaint. The street landscaping was new but it was good — it helped to recall the old green ambience and sense of seclusion and escape from the concrete jungle of the city.

But there were a few things no longer to be seen. The luxuriant old Singapore cherry trees which the kids used to climb and the sparrows that chattered happily in them. The old-fashioned manually-lit gaslight lamp-posts with their warm rays and discreet gaps of darkness that turned the evening Emerald Hill into a lovers' lane. The fiery red road-side fire-hydrants which never failed to stimulate the neighbourhood dogs to dehydrate. The black rubbish bins which also served as vessels for the seventh moon offering of burning joss-paper to the hungry ghosts. Sue Ann even felt nostalgia for the ruins of Number 106, that half-bombed house at the end of her block, now demolished and rebuilt.

She resented the intrusion of the few post-war blocks of terrace houses (though to their credit they did try considerately to look as inconspicuous as they could). And she detested the lone alien, that apartment block that managed to rise up triumphantly before the heritage lobby could save in its entirety the national treasure that is old Emerald Hill.

The old-fashioned cosy *kopi tiam* (coffee-shop) which served the best freshly-ground coffee on this side of heaven was gone. So too was the Chinese *kedai*, that provision-shop near the Hullet Road junction which was the Hill's own mini-supermarket. And where had all those friendly itinerant hawkers gone that brought their tasty treats right up to your door-step? Gone, like so many other good things of the past, gone beyond recall.

But she herself was not gone. Here she was, good as new, back from an age ago. Walking about the Hill, haunting it like ye olde ghost of Emerald Hill (and that's another legend lost!). Invisible like a spirit. A non-person. Yes, indeed a non-person to the men she passed — they hardly gave her a glance.

Sue Ann found that invisibility to men particularly depressing.

In the old days when she and the other girls of Nan-mei-su walked down Emerald Hill, all masculine eyes would be a-sparkle with the light of lively interest in them and they could always feel that inner glow of *joie de vivre* that ignites from such spontaneous combustion.

She caught a glimpse of herself in a window reflection. It was not that she had become decrepit. On the contrary she was still good to look at, albeit many moons had passed since her Emerald Hill heyday. She still had her girlish figure. How many of the other old Nan-mei-su girls could boast of that, she challenged? In her deprived childhood she had been underfed and was a bag of bones. She was saved by the Nan-mei-su food (left-over food really, but still good food, hard to come by during the War years). That food had put flesh on her starved frame and thereafter she had remained shapely through the years.

Her face remained much the same, her dark complexion concealing and softening the ravages of time better than those dainty fair faces whose loveliness out-shine but also out-wilt.

Yes, she still looked pretty. Despite that defect. What defect? A tiny thing really, nowadays always well camouflaged by her hair — that missing bit of her right ear lobe!

That bit of herself had been sliced off in one terrifying moment, the worst in her life, as she struggled vainly with the insane assailant out to maim her. And it could have been worse...

Sue Ann fingered the hidden mutilation. The trauma had faded long ago, the nightmare had been exorcised by time. The cold memory still remained.

It had happened here in Emerald Hill, in the backlane behind this very row of houses. Right here.

On that night of unforgettable terror. That psycho, Ang Bin, had chased her, his eager knife gleaming lustily, caught her, held that knife over her face and carved that disfigurement on her.

Yet he had been kind. Indeed he had been more than that to her... Is it true what they say, love and hate are two sides of the same coin? It certainly seemed so in his case.

With a shrug Sue Ann deliberately switched off on Ang Bin who would always remain an enigma in her life.

She now thought of the happiest days of her life, her spring of first love. She thought of the time she walked down the Hill with her hand in his. He was her first boyfriend, although a taboo boyfriend. That was indeed forbidden love but oh! so romantic, so sweet, so powerful — but so short. That whole affair had a quality of ephemeral magic about it, a kind of fast dream-world sequence. And it ended on a note that spirited her into the realms of sheer surrealism...

Unconsciously her fingers caressed the battered old silver cross she wore around her neck like some precious antique. It was indeed precious, doubly precious with cherished memories, precious as last gifts from two loved ones both dead and gone.

Yes, she belonged to Emerald Hill.

And Emerald Hill must belong to her. She now felt an overwhelming desire to possess the house, once her happy home and sanctuary. The owner must sell it to her. No one else must have the house. She would pay him any price he cared to name. She was not poor any more.

Sue Ann recalled her first pay-day at Nan-mei-su.

Soon as she got home to her Ulu Pandan attap hut, even before she could take off her shoes, Ma grabbed her purse in her rough way and snatched off her entire pay-packet, throwing back only a few dollars to her for pocket-money.

"Get food. Get clothes. Get house. What for you want money?" Ma rasped out. She gave her step-daughter no face at all. So what if the stupid girl had become the main bread-winner of the house? It was her duty to support her mother.

She caught Sue Ann's face looking unhappily at her.

" *Gong cha-boh* ! What for you just stand there like wood! So many things to do in the house, still don't go and do!"

The girl's face always annoyed her — that face which her stupid husband had once in an unguarded moment, praised as beautiful like her natural mother's.

Sue Ann worshipped her father, obeyed his every word. As for her step-mother, she never knew how to cope with her. Despite all ill-treatment she continued doggedly to try to be a filial daughter. Fortunately, she inherited from her father his virtues of endless patience and resilience, which helped. Her own Ma had persuaded her father to send her to the Convent school where the nuns taught her to expect suffering in this world, "this vale of tears", and also God's uncompromising commandment to "honour thy father and thy mother", which also helped.

After her own Ma died and her father remarried this terrible woman, her father was around for a while to ward off the bullying from Ma (she even obediently called the witch that cherished name when her father told her to do so!).

After her father died, Ma dropped all restraint. Sue

Ann was pulled out from school and put to work, washing clothes for the rich families along Holland Road, selling cakes at the market, growing vegetables and raising chickens, all the while getting regular beatings from Ma for the slightest provocations, real or imagined.

Sue Ann grew up with one constant fear, one nightmare, the image of Ma, arm raised high with a stick in hand, arm brought flailing down in terrible blow after blow. At such times, Sue Ann learnt to protect her face as in those mad moments, Ma seemed determined to attack that face which had once so warmed her late husband's heart.

So step-mother and step-daughter lived on unhappily, forced to stay on together by circumstances. For the woman bore no children of her own and so Sue Ann was a necessary evil to her, a constant irritant but nevertheless her meal-ticket and general servant. She herself didn't like to work, she preferred to play mahjong and cards with her cronies and gamble as she had done in those better days when her husband was still alive.

Then came the Japanese Occupation. And Ma heard about the money a neighbour's niece was able to earn as a waitress at a Japanese comfort house called Nan-mei-su...

In due course Sue Ann confided her home problems to Doris and May, who had become her best friends.

"Come stay my house," offered May. "Like that kind, what for to go home! You don't got to, you know?"

"No, I got to..."

"*Bodoh!*" Doris called her a fool and snorted impatiently. "She treats you like rubbish and you still say you got to go back!"

"My father asked me! He said: look after her... And love her. Love her for my sake. On his death-bed, he asked me. And I promised him."

"I don't understand you, Sue Ann. You crazy or what? She beats you up and you still go back. And *lagi!* (on top of that!) you go and give her all your money?" May was exasperated.

"But now she don't beat me no more, only scold one!"

"What you do when you go home?" Doris asked though she knew very well what the answer would be.

"Oh, plenty. Clean house, wash clothes, pluck vegetables, feed chickens. Ma has a sister. She helps us part-time. During week-days only. So I must work on Sunday..."

"You know what? You just too good to be true, Sue Ann!" concluded May, giving up.

"Next week you come home early!" Ma commanded Sue Ann one week-end.

"Why?"

"What you mean, why? Because Ma says so, that's why!"

"Ma, Please tell me. I big girl now."

When that did not work, she added: "If they ask me why, I must say why, or else sure cannot get come home early kind, what?"

"I want you meet Oh Kow."

"Oh Kow? Who Oh Kow?"

"Your cousin."

"That fellow! Don't want, Ma! What for to meet him? Everybody say he's a mad fellow, real *gila-gila* kind. Fierce like hell. Everybody knows he's gangster-chief. In his *kampong* (village) they all *takut* (fear) him like hell. And they all say he's always *gila-urat* (crazy) about girls!"

"That's why, lah! That's why they want you, stupid! His Pa want our help. He want Oh Kow settle down. He want him get married. He want find obedient wife, somebody look after Oh Kow, somebody young and can born kind, to born his children... He want you."

Sue Ann was struck dumb, horrified at the idea.

"He very rich, you know," Ma came out with the good news. "You know where we live next time? In his Pa's big, big house! And you no need work any more. No need Nan-mei-su. Real good luck for us, huh? Heaven really good to us!"

"Don't want, Ma! What for I go and marry that *samseng* (gangster)? Eee! People say he got VD!"

"Don't be stupid girl. I say you marry him, you marry him, you understand?"

"I don't want leave Nan-mei-su!"

Ma considered using the old stick on Sue Ann but thought better of it. Sue Ann had put on meat and she was no longer puny, in fact she looked so strong she might just turn the tables on her.

Then a grave suspicion sprang to Ma's mind.

"Why you like your Nan-mei-su so much? You got boyfriend there, ah?"

Sue Ann denied it. But the more she did so, the more Ma believed it must be so, otherwise why would the stupid girl deny it again and again.

Sue Ann finally gave up.

"You must got boyfriend there!" Ma said for the umpteenth time.

"OK, yes! You want me say so, I say so. OK, Ma, yes!" said Sue Ann.

"You say yes!" Ma was triumphant. "I knew it. You admit at last... Who he?"

"Don't know! Don't know what to say."

"My heaven! Not, not Japanese devil, is it?"

Sue Ann could not help enjoying the shocked look in her step-mother's eyes. On a rare perverse impulse, she nodded her head vigorously.

Ma had to sit down to take this in.

"And he big shot," Sue Ann expanded the fiction with wicked inspiration. "And he sure very angry if he hear you want me marry another man."

"He marry you?" Ma probed, her calculative mind beginning to work on the possibilities of the new situation.

Sue Ann was caught off-guard. She thought fast.

"No, he not ready yet... thinking about how to. Got problems, you know. Not so easy, you think what? He got to get special OK from Army. So I got to wait."

What a tangled web of lies it's becoming, thought Sue Ann perspiring as she realised how complicated all this was going to turn out. She wished she really had a Japanese boyfriend.

Ma wanted to meet him of course but Sue Ann said no, he would not agree, not until he could clear his hurdles with the Army.

When Sue Ann told the story to her two close friends, their immediate reactions surprised her. They laughed till they cried.

"You real genius, Sue Ann!" Doris proclaimed.

"You sure fixed your Ma's plans for good!" May concluded.

"I don't know..." Sue Ann was less confident. "Ma never give up easy. I know her. When I go home, bet you she just keep on nag and nag non-stop. Must meet my boyfriend kind. So, sure she going dig everything out from me. I sure say something wrong and she sure find out I tell lie only..."

Sue Ann was right. Ma started grilling her the minute she came home the next week-end. Sue Ann had a rough time fending off all her questions. She insisted that her boyfriend had made her promise not to tell anyone, not even her mother. He regarded the whole matter as a military secret.

Ma would not let off at all. She gave the girl no peace. In the end the poor girl capitulated completely and promised to bring her boyfriend home next week-end.

Back at Emerald Hill, Sue Ann was almost in tears in her desperation. Her two friends reassured her. Not to worry, they would help her out. They would think of something.

Doris said confidently, "I got good idea. But must think first. I tell you if OK, can work."

Mama-san listened with unbelieving ears as Doris told her Sue Ann's story and asked her for help. For Doris's solution depended on whether Mama-san could enlist a cooperative Japanese officer to pose as Sue Ann's lover.

"Poor Sue Ann!" Mama-san sighed.

But she did not hesitate at all. Of course she would

help. She began at once to check over the likely candidates for consideration. They had to be sporting enough, willing to help out with Sue Ann's problem, able to act the part with reasonable credibility, and if possible young and good-looking too. Mama-san put in a lot of effort sieving out impossible and improbable candidates. She believed in doing a good job, especially when it comes to helping one of her girls.

Finally she picked a young, handsome, athletic-looking Navy Lieutenant with laughing eyes and a friendly disposition. His name was Hayashi Santaro but his friends called him by his nickname which was "Momotaro-san" after a Japanese children's folklore hero.

"Any mother would be happy to have Momotaro-san for son-in-law!" Mama-san declared to Doris as she revealed her choice.

"And he will help?"

"Yes, he's most willing! Momotaro-san has seen Sue Ann around in the club. He's ready to do what he can for her. He's a good boy. I know his family in Kyoto. He's well brought up. Reliable. No monkey business..."

"He's Navy officer? Will be here long enough?" Doris asked.

"Yes, his ship's here a while for repairs. After he helps to solve Sue Ann's problem, he'll be gone with his ship. So, no problems. Neat and tidy, *neh*?"

Doris agreed it was a good choice.

Mama-san left it to Doris to talk to Sue Ann.

"How can?" Sue Ann blushed at the idea.

"Why not? It's only way, what? Your step-mother

believe you, and you OK, no need to marry that gangster fellow!"

"You mean, we purposely go out together and let people see kind? And then I take him home for Ma to meet him?"

"And you must pretend pretend be lovers, of course!" May chipped in. "That part *amboi!* Real nice part, what? Doris and I saw him already. Handsome like hell, boy! Sure wish I in your shoes, man!"

That only made Sue Ann even more embarrassed, until she turned all red despite her slightly dark skin.

Her two friends persuaded her to meet Momotaro-san. They also pointed out that it was she who had created her Japanese lover, and now her step-mother would never let her off until she produced him — so there was just no other way out.

And so Sue Ann went to meet Momotaro-san. They met in Mama-san's private lounge at Nan-mei-su.

Sue Ann blushed again and again. She had expected to feel shy but not so overwhelmed.

Momotaro-san was indeed good-looking with his bright and clear eyes, his fair and shining complexion, his white and even teeth, his pure white uniform. Every bit a white knight ready to rescue a damsel in distress, like in the English story books Sue Ann read in her Convent school.

Chemistry was absolutely right between them. So Sue Ann's heart throbbed with excitement and she stood there unable to say anything. And Momotaro-san, normally quick-witted and full of jokes, was equally bashful. The two remained tongue-tied before each other.

Mama-san laughed and said something in Japanese to Momotaro-san, obviously egging him on to start.

Then she said to Sue Ann, "I have to go out. The Colonel's waiting for me. I'll leave you two now. Work out your plans. I've explained everything to Momotaro-san. He'll do whatever you want. You can speak to him in English. He can understand it quite well."

They stayed silent for a full minute more after Mama-san left. Then they both suddenly spoke up at the same time. They had a good laugh over that. That helped to break the ice.

As they talked, Sue Ann warmed up to the young officer. He was shy but understanding, a stranger and yet so ready to help her. He, on his part, felt his heart melting with sympathy for this poor ill-treated girl, so sweet and innocent and alone in the world.

And over the next few days they met and talked and talked. The kindly Mama-san gave Sue Ann time off. And as planned they walked about together in Emerald Hill and around Orchard Road so that they might be seen.

"Sorry to request, but maybe we better walk closer?" he suggested. She shyly agreed.

After a while, "I think we better hold hands, no? Just for people to see, OK?" he ventured.

Again she readily agreed.

Their hands touched. She shook hers free almost at once, feeling the electricity of his touch shooting right up to her racing heart.

Their hands touched again. This time they did not let go. Even when they got back to the privacy of Mama-san's flat which had become their rendezvous. By then both knew what was going on inside themselves. For when they had to part they found it so hard even just to let go of their joined hands.

Still, they did not dare to give name to what they felt. But the next evening Momotaro-san tried.

"Sue Ann, I have to say something — " he began.

"No, don't say — " Sue Ann stopped him. She was not yet ready. She just wanted to carry on. Nothing must spoil it. This euphoric make-believe which was so real and yet with no a need to worry about rules, taboos, reputation, consequences.

That week-end Sue Ann brought her Japanese boy-friend to meet her step-mother.

They arrived in a Nan-mei-su car borrowed from Mama-san. As they came into the house hand-in-hand no play-acting was necessary. The old lady could see it plainly: they were a couple in love.

Momotaro-san was good. He suffered through the awkward difficulties of trying to communicate with an illiterate and unlikeable woman who understood only the Hokkien dialect which he did not speak, a woman whose feelings were a violent hotch-potch of fear, bravado, awe, hostility, avarice, wonder, frustration.

The first phrase she came up with was a standard opener for all local folks who had the good fortune to meet with a friendly Japanese.

"Master, *tabako aru ka*?" ("got any cigarettes?").

Momotaro-san emptied his pockets and gave her his entire stock.

Sue Ann protested but could not stop her from trying for more. Indeed Ma ordered her to be her interpreter.

"Ask him get me Nanboku whiskey also. And more cigarettes. And rice, too. And anything more?..."

"Ma, don't be so greedy kind, can or not? He get

fed up, then you know!"

"Ask him when he marry you."

"Ma, I already told you, what? He got to wait for OK."

And so it went on.

Momotaro-san sensed that Sue Ann was having a difficult time. He looked at his watch, pointed to it and to Sue Ann and himself and signalled to the old woman they had to leave. She was not yet finished with her shopping list. She wanted them to stay. She tugged at his sleeve. He had to shout at her rudely in Japanese.

"Yameyo, bakayaro!"

Ma respected that. She gave up.

Up to that point things had gone fairly smoothly and Sue Ann was glad though uncomfortable.

Then trouble started. Big trouble.

As Momotaro-san was about to get into the car after Sue Ann, a gang of five tough-looking characters suddenly appeared. Leading them was Sue Ann's cousin, Oh Kow. Big and ugly. Half-drunk. And in his right hand he brandished a crowbar.

A curious crowd materialised from nowhere as word had gone around swiftly that Oh Kow was drunk and spoiling for a fight. An entertaining free show could be expected.

"So, here's our great Jap lover. And his little tramp!" Oh Kow snarled. "They told me at the bar my rival has come. Come to meet his future mother-in-law. So, I've come too. Come to see for myself..."

Then addressing Sue Ann's step-mother he snarled out something vulgar and asked, "Auntie, come on, tell me the truth, you really want this Japanese devil instead of me?"

Auntie quickly exonerated herself.

"What can I do? That stupid girl don't listen to her Ma! Just do what she want!"

And with that she started cursing Sue Ann loudly for shamelessly selling herself to a Japanese devil, embellishing her sentiments with choice Hokkien vulgarities (which, just as well, defy translation). All this was also for the benefit of her neighbours. She had to watch her standing with them.

"So, Auntie, you agree? We finish off this Japanese devil?" Oh Kow asked Ma.

"You say the word, Auntie. We kill him off. His life is in your hands... My temple medium has given me a spirit no one can defeat. Today I fight anybody, I win! Just say the word!"

Sue Ann looked with fear in her Ma's direction. Her eyes pleaded with her. For the out-numbered Momotaro-san. His life was indeed in her hands.

"*Pah! Pah!*" Ma suddenly screeched out that notorious "attack!" call of gangsters. Sue Ann watched in voiceless horror, her entire being paralysed with fear.

Momotaro-san did not understand any of the words which were spoken in Hokkien. But he understood the situation, and what Oh Kow was about to start off. His adrenaline flow steeled him. It was not going to be easy. One against five. Maybe more, if the crowd joined in. His victory had to be swift and total against his first assailants, then exit *hayaku!* (pronto!) while the rest were in shock and disarray. Yet he had to be careful not to kill with his deadly hands. Death would definitely result in a Kempeitai investigation. Anything could happen then. Sue Ann might be blamed, there's no telling with the Kempeitai!

He began his mental preparations for karate.

"Now, let's see how good you are with men instead of girls!" Oh Kow snarled.

He and his men moved menacingly towards Momotaro-san.

Sue Ann watched petrified in the car, thinking only of her Momotaro-san's peril. He looked so puny facing the five heavily-built ruffians.

Momotaro-san moved clear from the car. He did not want Sue Ann hurt. He crouched slightly. His body became a controlled machine, tense, tightly coiled up, ready to spring. His hands assumed the classic perpendicular stance. His eyes took in his five attackers, sizing who would make the first move, who the second, who would hold back.

Oh Kow lurched forward with his crowbar held high over his head. To Momotaro-san, he was easy meat. Even before he had taken a couple of steps Momotaro-san suddenly lept forward to meet him.

"YAAAAAK!"

Momotaro-san let out a blood-curdling samurai cry and lunged out with a sledge-hammer straight punch that smashed Oh Kow's front teeth and sent him sprawling back dazed and out of action for the evening. His temple spirit had failed him.

Two others now closed in on Momotaro-san, one on each side. He kicked off one with a dynamite flying leg-blow that finished him off decisively as he fell and hit his head against a tree, blood later to ooze out copiously from his ears.

In the same split second Momotaro-san turned and met the other man with a sten-gun series of telling open-hand blows all over his body. The latter dropped like an unsupported sack, an idiotic look of puzzlement fixed on his face.

The remaining two men stood there stunned by the swiftness and utterness of the defeat of their three friends.

Momotaro-san moved towards them, eyes big and fierce, snorting somewhat like a raging bull, ready for more.

"*KOI!*" he yelled, inviting them to come on.

Instead, they turned and ran off.

Momotaro-san dusted his hands, straightened his jacket, bowed with dignity to Sue Ann's step-mother and said, "*Sayonara!*"

The crowd stood silent in shock. They made way for him and his car.

He got in with one very starry-eyed girl and drove off.

The emotional stress, the terror of watching her Momotaro-san in mortal danger stripped Sue Ann bare of all inhibitions. She loved her Momotaro-san passionately that very moment and she did not want to hide it any more. She could not.

As they drove off she sat still. Until they were clear from the village vicinity and in the loneliness of Farrer Road. Then she held back no longer. She leaned over and hugged and kissed him with abandon and he had to stop the car.

He was now totally exhausted. Delayed reaction to the toll taken by the fight. He leaned back and relaxed in sweet surrender to the heavenly bliss of Sue Ann's aggression of love, for the moment no more strength in him to respond in love.

Soon strength returned.

Happiness was not to be theirs for long.

One of Oh Kow's thugs was admitted to hospital and died from a skull fracture. The police investigated. They heard an unclear story about a fight between a Japanese and some villagers. They decided they should notify the Kempeitai.

Once word got around that the dreaded Kempeitai were coming, many people quickly disappeared from Ulu Pandan. Oh Kow and his friends were the first to go. It was too risky to hang around with the distinct prospect of being hauled in by the Kempeitai.

And about this time Sue Ann's step-mother disappeared too. Perhaps she too felt the Kempeitai might detain her for her role though only secondary and purely supportive.

Momotaro-san knew he could also be in trouble. He had failed to report to the Kempeitai a heinous crime, an attack on a Nipponjin. This was a sin as mortal as such an attack. He had not reported it because he did not want to make trouble for Sue Ann or her Ma. Also he had not expected any of those tough-looking gangsters to die from the fight. After all he had only handed out a few blows.

Mama-san's Colonel told her about the Ulu Pandan incident and the aftermath, how the gangsters concerned had vanished and the mysterious samurai had not turned up to report to the Kempeitai. She at once alerted Momotaro-san.

He was in a quandary. Would the Kempeitai track him down? How long would they take to do that? He remained undecided what to do. His worry was that no one ever knew how the Kempeitai would react. It was quite possible they might decide to punish Sue Ann as well. He could not take the chance.

Then the decision was taken out of his hands. He received his sailing orders. His ship's repair had been completed and his respite in *Syonanto* (as Singapore was then called) was over. And so too his brief time with the love he had found.

Sue Ann would never forget the agony of their hasty farewell in Mama-san's flat. Both were heart-sick as only young lovers forced to part so soon could be. They could not even promise to write, as Momotaro-san was going into active operation and his whereabouts would be secret.

Nevertheless, Momotaro-san promised her solemnly he would find some way to contact her as soon as he could do so.

She decided to give him the most precious thing she had. Her silver cross on a necklace of cord, a dull and battered thing with her own Mother's name "Mary" engraved on the back. It was her one sentimental belonging. Her Mother had given it to her, put it around her neck, on her sick-bed shortly before she died.

Sue Ann explained to her lover the strange personal story which made that cross so special to her.

Her Mother had smiled when Sue Ann started to polish the cross with her hanky minutes after receiving the gift. She told her not to worry about the cross looking so dull. It could be that her diabetic sweat made it so. She then went on with a prophetic statement spoken with such deliberation that Sue Ann could not help but recall it again and again later: When all was fine and happy again the cross would become shiny and bright once more.

When her Mother died Sue Ann took off the cross and kept it under her pillow. It was not proper to wear jewelry while in mourning. Each night when she looked at it she cried till through her tears the cross seemed even more dull and grey as though it was clouded over in sympathy with her grief of bereavement.

But on the seventh day after her Mother's death, that customary day for departed souls to visit their families, even as Sue Ann kissed and looked steadily at her cross, the dullness receded and before her eyes it became shiny! And she knew that God in his goodness had allowed her Mother to reach out to tell her she was now happy in heaven.

"Keep this with you, Momo. Always," she said as she took it from her neck and hung it around his.

"*Hai* (Yes), Sue Ann. Your cross will always be with me. As long as I live, Sue Ann."

"Don't forget, you must find a way to reach me."

"*Hai!*"

"And let me know where you are."

"*Hai!*"

"And how you are..."

"I promise," Momotaro-san's eyes told Sue Ann that that was a vow he was determined to keep, come what may.

And yet she continued to feel that heavy burden of heart, that ominous premonition that this was to be the last time they would be together...

The Kempeitai never came to question Sue Ann. She did not know why. It must have been easy to trace her connection. After all the duel was over her. Perhaps something more important turned up and they dropped the matter. Perhaps Mama-san's Colonel knew more than he showed and he had got the case closed out of consideration for Mama-san and her friends. Sue Ann would never know.

Life is full of question marks and loose ends.

Momotaro-san never wrote. There was only silence. What had happened?

"He's right there in the middle of the war, you know? How can he sit down and write letters?" Doris reasoned.

"You know soldiers, cannot tell anyone where they are. Sure, must be secret, what?" May suggested.

"But so long already, so many months! And he promised... " Sue Ann protested, holding back her tears.

And then in a softer voice, full of renewed faith: "He'll keep his promise, you wait and see. Sure he will. I know."

When several more months passed by without any news and Sue Ann pined away each day in gloomy hope, Doris and May discussed with Mama-san and the three decided the time had come to help their friend face the harsh possibilities of the situation.

"Sue Ann, better not expect and expect only! You are not dumb, you know his chances not good... " Doris began.

Sue Ann sat quiet for a while. Then she sighed a sigh of despair.

"Yes," she admitted dully, "maybe you right. How can so many months no news. Can't be good! He never do that to me... Unless, unless something, something bad happened... "

"Sue Ann," Mama-san spoke gently, "I'm sorry. I tell you from my heart. I don't think he's still alive... The war is going against us. So many Japanese ships have been sunk. If he's still alive, surely he would have written. Not a single word, not to you, not to his friends here. Even his parents in Kyoto don't have news... "

"That's right, Sue Ann," May joined in blunt as usual. "Face it. *Sudah mati-lah!* (Dead already!) Gone. No more. You won't see him again. So just get up. Go on with your own life."

Sue Ann broke down. Her friends let her cry on. She had to let it all out, once and for all. That was the idea of telling her frankly, brutally.

"You promised, you promised, Momo... " she kept on repeating in between her sobbing.

"I must know for sure!" Sue Ann appealed to Mama-san.

"I've tried. I'll keep trying. There's a lot of confusion now. Too many casualties. And morale is very low with everybody. It's getting hard to find out things..."

"Life full of questions with no answers, Sue Ann. No use worry worry all the time. We just got to live on, that's all!" Doris came in. She spoke for herself too, thinking of her Ah Lek.

"Dear God, I got to know for sure, please let me know for sure!" Sue Ann cried out.

Her friends left her in Mama-san's flat to spend the night. Mama-san thought it a good idea for her to be left alone for a while. To come to terms with herself, to accept the inevitable. She let her sleep in her lounge which was more private than the Emerald Hill rooms shared with so many.

Sue Ann stayed awake deep into the night. Her

friends' counsel started to make sense painful though it was. But she still could not accept Momo failing to try to reach her. He had promised her. And she knew he would not disappoint her. She felt something missing, some vague thing unfulfilled.

"Dear God," she prayed, "and my dear Mother in heaven, help me! Please let me know, I have to know, where he is. And how he is... Is he still alive? Sailing around on a ship? Or captured? Or ship-wrecked somewhere? Or dead and in Heaven with you? Please, God, let me know!"

She fell into a fitful sleep. She woke up with a start as though someone had called her up. She felt a sudden thirst that had to be quenched, a burning dryness in her throat. She got up to get a drink from the tap.

She peeped into Mama-san's room where the bathroom was. The good woman was snoring away. She did not want to disturb her, so she decided to go downstairs to the club restaurant toilet.

The club was eerie in its half-dark quietness. So noisy at most times in the daytime it now resembled a deserted graveyard with unexpected shadows here and there like body-less spirits of the thousands who had once made merry in that place and now lie still in so many battlefields all over the Pacific, victor-victims of their meaningless war.

Sue Ann went into the toilet. It was bright enough from the lamp-post outside. She did not turn on the light. She drank the refreshing water. It roused her up to wakefulness.

From the corner of her eyes, she had seen something vague, something vaguely familiar, on the sink ledge. Now her less drowsy eyes had time to focus on it. They opened wide in utter amazement as she took it in.

Impossible! How could it be? Who could have left it there?

It was her old battered silver cross, the "Mary" at the back confirming the fact.

But moreover it now glittered bright. Joyfully shiny. Like on that other occasion, that seventh day after her Mother's death when happiness shone out of it to convey its consoling message.

"Momo!" Sue Ann called out in a loud whisper as she looked around in wonder.

But she did not really expect to find him around. She knew he was not there with her.

And yet, she knew he was. And always would be.

"Thank you, Momo!"

CHAPTER THREE

Second Love

And what of Oh Kow and Sue Ann's step-mother? For a while the girls of Nan-mei-su heard nothing of them.

And no news was good news. For when the girls got news, it was with a vengeance. Vengeance with a capital V.

The news came from an unexpected source. A school-mate of May's, now married to a farmer. She came whispering news that Oh Kow and his gang were hiding in her area, rural Paya Lebar, in the midst of the maze of attap huts there. In fact right next to her own hut. And so near it was that at night she could hear them arguing, cursing and swearing.

And what's more, Sue Ann's step-mother was with them.

She had to earn her keep. She had to work for the gangsters, serve them hand and foot as their cook and servant. It was not an easy life for her. She hated it.

She grumbled to her neighbours, blaming all her troubles on that stupid step-daughter of hers prostituting herself to the Japanese. She had become a thing of pure venom, railing against Sue Ann day and night.

May's friend came to warn May, Sue Ann and the other Nan-mei-su girls. Two nights ago she had overheard Sue Ann's step-mother and the gangsters talking to a stranger who had come to visit Oh Kow. The whole lot of them had been drinking away and the stranger sounded particularly violent and dangerous. The gangsters had recounted a garbled version of their heroic fight with Sue Ann's Japanese boyfriends (who suddenly became plural, and quickly almost legion). Following which the old lady chipped in with her customary litany of loud imprecations against the stupid girl who had caused all their troubles.

"That stupid girl and her friends, so no shame! Sell themselves to Japanese devils. Somebody must teach them lesson!" she concluded piously.

"Ang Bin here can! He can teach them. He do it for you. He hates Japs like hell! They killed his father, you know," Oh Kow offered on his friend's behalf.

"Do what?" the old lady asked.

"In China they cut off their ears," the stranger spoke with obvious relish. It was a frightening voice, sadistic with a ring of the insane in it. Dangerous compared to the old lady's hot-air hysterics and the gangsters' vitriolic curses and snarls.

"Cut off her ear? Mess up that face? Heh! Heh! Heh! I like that!" the old crone cackled away. "Yes, cut off her ear! And cut up her face, too, please! She always think she pretty one, after that day her stupid father said her face pretty... Yes, yes, that's good. Cut off her ear! And also cut up those other girls. Give it to them good!"

"OK, Ang Bin do it for you. Right, Ang Bin? You do it? For your father? For revenge," Oh Kow urged his friend and roared out his pleasure at the thought. The others joined in with their raucous laughter, the old witch's voice high and shrill in her evil ecstasy.

"You promise, Ang Bin?" Oh Kow demanded.

"What you want? I cut off a cock's head and swear on it?"

"Yes, sure! Why not? Do it proper. Tomorrow! You cut the cock's head. In front of your father. His picture. Swear in his name," Oh Kow insisted.

"Sure!" Ang Bin agreed.

May's friend peeped out, trying to get a good look at Ang Bin as he was leaving. But his back was to her and he walked off fast and all she could see was that he was a young man probably around thirty or so, of average height and he walked with a slight roll and swagger rather like a seaman. And his face must have been red, judging by the back of his neck — and his name.

May's friend's news naturally frightened Sue Ann. The next morning she was terrified of going out. As she had to go to work, the other girls decided to escort her to Nan-mei-su in full force and that morning the residents of Emerald Hill were treated to a special procession of pretty girls in the white Nan-mei-su uniforms. But the procession was over very quickly. For Sue Ann was so scared she made everybody jog practically all the way.

Who could blame her? For any young girl the prospect, suspense and terror of physical maiming must surely be petrifying. Even worse than that classical calamity for maidens referred to genteelly as a fate worse than death.

However there was one silver lining, one tiny consolation. The abrupt intervention of pressing personal danger did help her to come out faster from her melancholia of mourning for her lost love.

Doris sought Mama-san's help.

"We must help Sue Ann, *neh!* Get her away to a safe place for a while. Out of *Syonanto*. Also, I'm going to report to the police. Must catch those gangsters," Mama-san declared decisively.

Doris agreed. Those dangerous hoodlums should be put away in jail.

"Better don't tell Sue Ann first. Wait till police catch them all. You know Sue Ann. She sure feel bad if police catch her Ma, too," Doris cautioned.

"How to get her away?" Doris worried.

As always, the resourceful Mama-san had the answer.

In Penang the *Oka-butai* (Oka Regiment) had an establishment somewhat like Nan-mei-su though on a smaller scale and for officers only. The Mama-san there had not been well and had been trying to get someone to cover her duties so she could go back to Japan for a break. Mama-san believed she could arrange for Doris and Sue Ann to go over and together cover the lady's duties for a month or two.

"But what about you, Mama-san? Who help you here?" Doris liked the idea a lot but she was concerned for Mama-san.

"It's OK, *neh!*" Mama-san smiled, "May is quite

good. She can help me. And Sleepy too. And also Lily. You two just go and take it easy in Penang. Not much work there, not so big and not popular, so very quiet and easy, *neh!* Just right for Sue Ann. You look after her there, talk to her, help her to forget Momo, *neh!*"

Doris held Mama-san's soft and generous hands, squeezing them. She knew her boss was giving up to them her own chance for a holiday on the beaches of Penang.

"*Arigato gozaimasu* (thank you), Mama-san!"

"No need for *arigato*, Doris. You know all of you like my own children, *neh*? Just go and have a good rest. And when you get back, those gangsters will be in jail. And I hope that Ang Bin as well. Even if he escapes, no need to worry. He'll be so busy hiding from the police... So it'll be safe again."

Sue Ann was told the news when she got back from Penang, refreshed and no more a nervous wreck.

The police had raided the Paya Lebar hide-out. Oh Kow and all his gang with him were now under detention. Ang Bin could not be traced but no doubt he was on the run with the police looking out for him.

Sue Ann's step-mother was lucky. She was away when the police raided the Paya Lebar hide-out. But she disappeared completely, no one knew where.

Life went back to normal, Sue Ann and the other girls quickly gaining confidence and once more walking the paths of Emerald Hill, Cairnhill and Orchard Road with usual aplomb.

Well, not exactly normal.

A couple of fresh distractions occurred to create new waves to forestall any humdrum in the lives of the girls.

One was that Sleepy, that perpetually half-asleep "baby" of the Nan-mei-su girls, suddenly woke up. And the stimulant was a boy, Billy the Kid, the teenage nephew of the club's Hainanese cook who had come to live with his uncle in his Nan-mei-su quarters.

The other development was more complicated and distressing. Mama-san's ex-boyfriend came back unexpectedly into her life, creating an uncomfortable triangular affair at the centre-stage of Nan-mei-su life.

There was yet another development, one that was intimate and personal to Sue Ann.

A new young man entered Sue Ann's life. Someone to become her second love.

Beng was a black marketeer. That was nothing heinous. In fact almost a respectable vocation during the Occupation when practically everybody took part in the black market in one way or another. Some, like Beng, dealt in more lines and made a full living from it. Beng bought and sold anything from medicine like MB693 to Straits Settlements dollar notes, Japanese cigarettes, and brandy.

Beng appeared on the scene looking for Sue Ann's step-mother. He claimed she owed him a few hundred dollars for some cigarettes she had taken from him. He asked to speak to Sue Ann on the Nan-mei-su phone and was referred to Doris instead.

Beng explained that he was trying to get Sue Ann's help to reach her step-mother. Doris told him sorry, Sue Ann had lost touch with her and would not be able to help him. Beng pleaded to be allowed to speak to Sue Ann himself. Together they might be able to pool what they knew and find out where the old lady was. Doris was not keen to help him.

Sue Ann happened to come in behind Doris and she overheard part of the conversation and gathered it was about her. She insisted on taking over the call.

She listened to Beng as he re-explained and urged her to meet him. Something in his quiet voice was compulsively beckoning. Sue Ann agreed to meet him at the Emerald Hill coffee-shop near the Hullet Road junction later that afternoon.

She had a premonition that something exciting was going to happen but she did not know exactly what it was.

Beng was a slim but wiry-looking young man with searching eyes and a determined jaw. He spoke sparingly, measuring out his words with careful consideration, all the time his eyes watching and analysing. Those clear eyes spoke a strength of character which reminded Sue Ann of her late lover, Momo. But there was also something in them that bespoke a troubled soul beneath the surface.

Sue Ann had liked him even before they met, now she felt eager to help him as far as she could. She told him she had not gone to her former Ulu Pandan home nor to her step-mother's Paya Lebar hide-out since the fight over her former boyfriend. So she had no information to give him. But if her Ma contacted her she would let him know. She doubted that he would get his money back.

A sudden thought occurred to her.

"You want I pay you?"

"No!" he denied firmly, "you don't owe me the money."

Sue Ann smiled, warming up to him, "If you need, I can pay you something."

Beng shook his head, his eyes steadily taking in her smile. She could feel him looking deeper into herself and seeing more than anybody else she had ever met before. She blushed for no apparent reason and she felt a little angry with herself for her confusion.

The business that had brought them together had concluded yet they lingered, both reluctant to separate. Beng seemed to sense Sue Ann's willingness to stay on and talk. He realised he had to take the initiative now to create a reason or excuse so that they might meet again.

"Maybe there's something you can do for me — " he began.

"Sure! Just tell me. I do it for you," she replied at once, perhaps a bit too fast for maidenly modesty.

"Maybe you can recommend some customers for my stuff."

"Sure! I can... Our girls also have things to sell," she replied happily.

And so the two continued to meet. Each time they took their time over business, each meeting lasting longer than the last.

They became friendly enough for her to invite him to a picnic a few of the girls were planning to have at the seaside at Katong.

They cycled there, some pedalling, some hitch-hiking side-saddle on the bar in front of the seat.

Beng carried Sue Ann on his bicycle.

The proximity of Beng's body, the feel of his strong arms around her, his heavier breathing at an up-slope, his faint but exciting masculine smell intoxicated her to euphoria — it was heaven to Sue Ann all the way to the hot beach and its passionate sea.

Beng, though phlegmatic as ever, seemed to enjoy the trip too, but he kept his peace and betrayed no emotion.

The other girls could read Sue Ann and they lost no opportunity to tease her.

Lily was being similarly transported on her boyfriend's bike and as they cruised by she yelled out for everybody's benefit:

"Hey, Sue Ann! Take it easy, man! No funny business, OK? Not night time, you know!"

"*Shiok sa-kali* (real pleasure), Sue Ann?" May contributed cheekily as she rode past them on her own bike. "Don't forget we're all going to Katong, huh?"

Even little Sleepy who was cycling side-by-side with Billy deliberately moved up to say loudly:

"Wah! Enjoy only, man! Some people so clever, come without bike. Next time I also know, man!"

Sue Ann blushed a lot but derived pleasure from all that ribbing.

Beng said nothing. He's so shy, thought Sue Ann. And she felt even more attracted to him.

They swam, they ate, they drank a lot of syrup water, they played games, they sang the Japanese songs they learnt at the club as well as the old community songs they learnt earlier in school, Clementine, Daisy Daisy, My Bonnie, Irish Eyes and all that jazz.

The ride back was in the moonlight. And in those days the streets were deserted at night — and utterly romantic as only Singapore night streets could be...

Lily and her friend rode dangerously, Lily distracting her beau with cuddles and kisses till he wobbled so often that he had to cry out for mercy.

Sleepy called out that she had a flat tyre and made Billy stop behind with her. How could she have a flat with her solid tyres, Sue Ann wondered. But she minded her own business.

Beng remained quiet. Still so shy, Sue Ann told herself. Or was it something else? Can't be! He responds when I touch him. But why, why doesn't he start off? Why doesn't he make any advances? Really too shy? Or what?

Sue Ann began to feel a little uneasy. Beng was too quiet. Throughout the day he had been quiet, even quieter than his usual.

"Beng," she began, then stopped, not knowing what to say next.

He did not respond at once. Sue Ann noticed the silence. She did not like it.

"Yes?" Beng asked belatedly.

"Beng, anything wrong?"

"What?"

"How come you so quiet one?"

"Sorry, Sue Ann. You know me, don't talk much."

"Is that it? Or — "

"Or what?"

"Nothing," Sue Ann did not dare to press him further for a clarification. In her heart there were many fears. She would not be able to bear it if Beng confirmed any of them. Perhaps it was happening too fast for him. Perhaps Beng's heart danced to a slower beat. She was on a rebound and perhaps her ricochet heart was shooting too hastily in Beng's direction.

Perhaps he had another girl? Perhaps he had many girls and was not ready to be committed to just one? Perhaps he was the confirmed bachelor type?

Sue Ann agonized over her many doubts, her

uncertainty of his love. He loves me? He loves me not? He loves me?

Then it happened.

A few evenings later when Beng had arranged to take her out on her night off, he stood her up.

She waited and waited. No sign of him. And no phone call either. Sue Ann rang up the bachelor flat which he shared with friends. They said he had been out all day. They did not know where he had gone. Yes, they would ask him to call her as soon as he came back. Did she imagine it or was someone sniggering in the background?

Sue Ann was almost in tears. Doris told her not to worry, there's probably a simple explanation, he might be caught up in some business deal, or he might even have forgotten the date. And Doris had to stop her phoning the hospitals straightaway to find out if he had an accident.

At about midnight, Sue Ann decided she had to go over to Beng's flat to wait for him. Lily and her latest boyfriend (she had already jilted or been jilted by the one that came to the picnic) drove her there and waited for her.

Sue Ann found Beng inside.

"I've just come back — " he said, eyes averted from hers.

"What happened? You know, you had me so worried – "

"I was busy. Caught up with business in Johore Bahru. Couldn't get to a phone. You shouldn't have worried."

Then all of a sudden it came. The brush-off. From

out of the blue, he said in a cool, flat and emotionless tone, "Anyway, it's better for you not to be mixed up with a person like me. I may as well be frank. I'm not what you think. I'm no good for you. For your own sake, please stay away from me!"

Sue Ann was deeply hurt. Beng noticed the pain.

"I'm sorry, Sue Ann," he softened. "I don't want to hurt you. I'm really not good for you!"

He looked away.

Sue Ann moved towards him. He edged off. Sue Ann stopped in her tracks, transfixed by the trauma of rejection. She held out her arms. They remained pitifully empty as he averted his eyes and turned his back on her.

His next word stabbed right into her aching heart. "Go!"

Tears welled up in her eyes. He did not see them.

"Better go back and sleep! It's too late now. We can talk tomorrow, another time... " Beng softened again but stayed firm.

Sue Ann left. But that tomorrow never came. Instead Sue Ann received a good-bye note from Beng.

He was very sorry he had misled Sue Ann into thinking they could be more than friends. That was just not possible for them, although he did find her very attractive. He was sorry he had not turned up for the appointment he had fixed. Yet, in another sense which Sue Ann would never know, he was not sorry for he would have done something very bad to her. Indeed the evil part of him had planned to do this bad thing when he arranged the date, so he was glad he could not go through with it.

Sue Ann sat there in a daze. First Doris took over and read the note. Then Lily, who was with them when a boy brought the note over.

"Wassa matter with that fellow?" Doris was puzzled. She was a good judge of people and she could see that Beng liked Sue Ann although he was obviously shy or something.

"Men! He loves you, Sue Ann," Lily concluded. "But he's sex maniac kind. You know, cannot control once he let himself go. That's what he says, isn't it? You read his letter. He says so, what?"

"I want to talk with him. Why can't he just meet me and talk?" Sue Ann wept.

And she tried again and again to reach Beng. Without success. Beng had moved out of his quarters. No forwarding address. No clue where he was going to. He was clearly avoiding Sue Ann.

But Sue Ann did not give up. She just could not believe that Beng did not feel for her. There was some dark secret he did not want to tell her. But she was determined to find out. Whatever the cost. She had to know. She felt that once everything was brought out into the open the whole matter would be resolved and the way would be clear for them to get together again...

So through the wide network of Nan-mei-su contacts, she and her friends passed the word around to look out for this young man, about thirty or so, slim but wiry, with searching eyes and a determined-looking jaw and a taciturn nature.

"Oh yes," added Lily to her bar-maid friends, "he walks like a man of power, like a dragon you know, not afraid of anything..."

"Don't worry, Sue Ann! We sure to find him!" Lily was confident. "His business sure to take him to bars. And we got so many friends in bars everywhere... "

Which proved to be absolutely correct, although there was a more straightforward reason why Beng now went to the bars. To drink. And to get drunk.

One evening Sue Ann received the news on the phone. Beng was spotted at the Joyance Bar in Geylang Road near the Gay World gambling stalls. (Now don't let your imagination run wild! The word "gay" had a perfectly straight and happy meaning in those days.)

Sue Ann was alone in the hostel. She decided she could not wait for Doris or the others. She had to get there straightaway, otherwise he might be gone. Geylang Road was a main thoroughfare and she could get there on one of those shared taxis that plied the route running on charcoal burners and steam. These picked up passengers at bus-stops and she could wait for one at the bottom of Emerald Hill.

She had to go at once and talk it out with Beng.

The night was well advanced by the time she reached the Joyance Bar. But there were not many customers around. She picked out Beng without difficulty.

But there was something very different about Beng now. Something in his appearance, in his demeanour.

He had already drunk quite a bit. His face, even in the subdued lighting, was an unusual colour, a strong red. And the expression on it was hard and angry. His personality had changed too. He was garrulous, talking even with no one at his booth.

"Beng!" Sue Ann came over to him and sat down in front of him.

He looked at her. He did not recognize her. But he

spoke to her obviously thankful for an audience.

"You know, they took him away. My poor old father. When they first came to Ipoh. He never came back. And my poor mother. She, she just cried till she became blind. Then she died, too. So I beat up some soldiers. So they wanted to catch me. So I ran away. To Singapore... "

Sue Ann listened intently. Beng had never spoken about his family tragedy. She reached out with her hand to touch him. He shook off her touch roughly. But he carried on talking without looking away from his glass of alcohol. Nanboku, that awful stomach-burning local whiskey made from fermented pineapple.

"And what do I find? A girl, a cute Singapore girl, but dammit! She's a Jap-lover! Shameless pros!" Beng suddenly became violent, sweeping off the empty bottle on his table with one hand and sending it crashing to the floor.

Sue Ann, taken aback by the sudden violence, listened in hypnotised fascination as Beng went on:

"Even her own mother asked me. Teach her a lesson, she said! Cut off her ear! And I took an oath on it. Cut off a cock's head on it. Swore to my father and my mother on it. I do it for them, cut off the girl's ear!.. Now I have to do it!"

Now Sue Ann understood. Beng's black secret. Stark terror quickly replaced shock in her heart. So Ang Bin is here at last. And he is Beng! Can this be real? Or just a crazy nightmare. Sue Ann's reeling mind became disorientated. She felt reality slipping away from her.

It was not fair... Ang Bin means "Red Face" in Hokkien and Beng's face was never red — until he got drunk. How could she know then that Beng was Ang Bin?

"Sue Ann," Beng now addressed her but as though she was not there in front of him. "Why? Why? So sweet and so terrible! Why sell yourself to a Jap devil?"

"I was forced to pretend... Then I fell in love − " Sue Ann involuntarily answered him, crying out in agony, not caring about the curious stares of the others in the bar.

"Forced? Pretend? Love?" Beng sneered out each word loud, getting up and bringing his frighteningly red face closer to Sue Ann with each word. Now his face was so close she could feel his panting hot breath and her heart began to beat faster too. Was it sheer fear? Was it the excitement of a very dangerous kind of passionate love that was ready to surrender to death? Or was it just an onset of madness?

Then he let out the full venom of the fury in every fibre of his being:

"SLUT!"

Tears of deep-heart hurt rushed up to her eyes. He was so close he could read them. He stared into her eyes. For a second Sue Ann thought she saw a flicker of hesitation in his eyes, perhaps a touch of compassion, but at once that was suppressed and the fiery anger returned.

She now felt nothing towards him, nothing except fear. She knew she must escape from this Beng, run back home as soon as she can.

"Ang Bin, ah, why you so angry kind? Why *bising-bising* (noisy) disturbing everybody only? Don't shout so much, can or not?" the lady-owner of the bar now came over and occupied Beng's attention for a moment.

Sue Ann seized her chance. She slipped out quickly. But even as she ran out of the door, she heard Beng yelling out to her and giving chase.

She hid behind a column in the five-foot-way. She saw Beng rushing by. She jumped into the open monsoon drain, peeping out to see if Beng had gone. Beng looked around for a while, then he apparently gave up. He caught a taxi and rode off.

Sue Ann got out of the drain. All she wanted now was to get home to Emerald Hill as fast as possible.

When her taxi dropped her at the foot of Emerald Hill, it was well past midnight and she hurried up the Hill. It was a moonlight night but so late that nobody was about.

As she passed the Singapore Chinese Girls' School not far from the bottom of the Hill she thought she heard someone following her. She looked around but saw no one. Silly! Imagination only, she thought.

But a few steps on, again she heard the footsteps behind her, this time it seemed more distinct.

Was it the ghost? She had heard about the ghost which haunted one of the Emerald Hill houses but she never believed in it. Could it be that there really was a ghost?

Sue Ann laughed to herself. Fancy believing in such stuff! She began whistling to herself a popular Japanese folk tune, "Kojo no tsuki" ("Moon over the deserted castle").

That did not help at all. In fact it made things worse. Her heart beat faster as she accelerated her stride up the Hill.

Then she heard the steps again. This time there was no mistake at all.

She turned around. She saw it! The shadowy figure. It was hurrying towards her!

She panicked. She ran. Fast as she could. The figure behind immediately gave chase.

Clop! Clop! Clop! Clop!

She reached the backlane behind the two blocks of shophouses opposite Hullet Road. Plenty of trees there, easier to hide, she thought. She turned into the backlane.

Her pursuer saw her and speeded up.

CLOP! CLOP! CLOP! CLOP!

The steps drew menacingly nearer. Her frantic desperation to rush away became her downfall. In her reckless hurry she tripped over some tree roots and fell. She tried to get up. Her legs collapsed under her. She gasped in sudden pain. She had twisted her ankle.

She could see the dark figure looming close. Her throat went dry. She opened her mouth to scream. No sound came out. Panic paralysed her vocal chords.

And the next second the hunt was over. She was cornered. The hunter stood triumphant over his petrified quarry.

In the pale moonlight, Sue Ann saw clearly the gleam of the knife in Ang Bin's hand as he now knelt over her, his eyes flashing as brightly as his naked blade.

"Now you pay the price, you Jap-loving slut!" Ang Bin snarled.

The cold knife closed in on Sue Ann's face.

"Beng!" she managed to whisper out from her almost voiceless throat.

Ang Bin paused.

"Beng..." she gasped out again.

"Don't call me that! I'm Ang Bin... "

"Beng!" she sobbed out the third time, her big wet eyes pleading beseechingly into her assailant's wild eyes.

"Don't, don't look at me like that!"

"Beng, Beng, Beng... " Sue Ann sensed somehow that her only chance lay in that desperate chant, the only word she could manage anyway.

"NO! I have to do this. I've sworn ... "

The tip of the knife now hovered over her cheek. Sue Ann tried again to scream but her throat now completely failed her. No sound came out. She could not even pant for dear life. Her heart, breath, life — everything stopped.

This is the end, she thought. Dear God, only you can save me!

Beng, Beng, Beng, she resumed in desperation the mental invocation of that name even as she sank into merciful unconsciousness.

When she opened her eyes again she thought she was in Heaven. She heard soft friendly voices calling her name. She smiled in response. But she was so exhausted she promptly fell asleep again. She heard some unfamiliar strange authoritative voice saying, "Let her rest now. The sleep will do her good. You can talk to her tomorrow."

The next morning when she woke up she felt this large bandage over the top part of her face. She saw she was safe in her bed at home now. That was a relief. But not for long. The events of the previous evening rushed back to her mind and her hands went at once to check her face. She confirmed with horror and dismay the bandage on her face. So Ang Bin did it!

"God! God!" she screamed.

Her scream brought her friends running into her room.

"My face! My face!" she sobbed, appealing to Doris with her unspoken question, clutching her hands tightly.

"It's all right, Sue Ann. It's OK. It's nothing!" Doris said.

"What you mean, nothing?"

Sue Ann insisted on taking off the bandage at once to see her face.

Only a tiny bit of her right ear had been sliced off. It had bled profusely but already a scar was forming.

"I'm ugly! No one will look at me!" Sue Ann moaned.

"Rubbish!" May scolded her. "Only a small small cut, what? Nothing at all, man! He could have cut off your whole ear!"

"You very lucky one! Lucky for you Beng came along. He saved you, you know?" Lily disclosed. "Ang Bin ready to cut you up real good! Cut off whole ear, sure thing, not just that *kechil - kechil* (tiny) bit! Your face sure gone case, man!"

"Beng saved me?" Sue Ann was confused.

"Yes, and you know he carried you here. In his arms. Your blood flowing all over him," Doris reported. "You should have seen him, man. Crying like baby, shirt wet with your blood and his sweat, cannot talk clearly what happened."

"He banged our door like mad! We opened it. There he was, looking like mad fellow. And you like dead in his arms... We thought you surely dead one!" Lily added.

"He brought me back? Beng carried me back? Beng? How can? It was him! He attacked me, he cut my face!"

"How can?" Doris echoed, puzzled. Sue Ann must still be in shock, she thought. "You mixed up, lah! Beng saved you. He brought you home! We asked him who attacked you. He told us Ang Bin! He knows Ang Bin, you know? He hates Ang Bin. He called Ang Bin bastard, swine, devil!"

Sue Ann suddenly felt too tired to argue. The world had gone crazy.

"He went to phone for doctor!" May remembered, adding, "funny, he never came back!"

"He talked to me before he went," Sleepy revealed. "Sorry, I forgot to say, Sue Ann. He said to tell you good-bye. And to say sorry. Oh yes, also to say Ang Bin is gone, out of your life. Forever! Will never *kachau* (disturb) you again."

CHAPTER FOUR

Chicken Love in the Nan-mei-su Kitchen

Sleepy was the "baby" of the Nan-mei-su girls. Barely in her teens she was the last to join the girls, a kind of Joannie-come-lately.

Plump with cuddly baby fat, with a shiny wax face, dimples and rosy cheeks, teenage pig-tails and cheeky eyes, she was the little sister of all the girls and the darling of Mama-san. Everybody was protective towards her. Including some (of course not all) of the men who came to Nan-mei-su. Sleepy reminded them of their daughters or little sisters at home. So, paradoxically she was more safe there than elsewhere in *Syonanto*, right there in the middle of a comfort house where the Japanese authorities provided sex (under reasonable control) in addition to food and drinks.

Quite soon after Sleepy's arrival one of the customers initiated a feeler, a groping attempt at assaulting the little girl. Mama-san came down on the poor man with such a quick-delivery of Japanese invectives that (as the story came to be told) the fellow slunk out of the club, tail between his legs, never to be seen or heard of by mankind again.

Then Mama-san told Sleepy that in future she was to say that she was Mama-san's own adopted daughter. That was what she should have told the unsuccessful molester and that would forestall any sanguine forays in future.

Mama-san would not allow Sleepy to work in the diner or (God forbid!) the bar. Her job was to do paper-work and she spent her time mostly in the kitchen, helping Uncle Foo the kindly Hainanese cook to work out his requisitions and occasionally helping the kitchen staff to chop vegetables and so on.

Uncle Foo had older women helpers who worked hard and so he could be easy on Sleepy. And so she would often be found in some corner, curled up with a book, usually a romantic story, but fast asleep.

And thus her nickname. The girls called her "Sleepy Head" at first but later this was shortened to just "Sleepy".

Sleepy was distantly related to Lily who introduced her to Mama-san for work. She came from a big family which lived with other big families. Hers resided in one of those big bungalows in Sophia Road that had seen better days but had degenerated into miniature townships what with the population explosions exploding unchecked in them.

Her absence from home was scarcely noticed by her huge family ("tribe" might be a more appropriate description), or rather her multitudinous siblings and their descendants (her dear parents having departed to their well-earned rest, exhausted after their enervatingly productive existence).

Sleepy enjoyed being a Nan-mei-su girl. Everyone was friendly, even Lily who would occasionally bully her the way some of her older sisters did at home. But this was something she expected and naturally accepted.

She cheerfully took all other things in her stride too, being of a lively and optimistic disposition, that is when not asleep over her book.

"She's still a growing child," Mama-san would say dotingly, restraining anyone from waking the girl up.

Of course Sleepy could and did see and hear some of the goings-on at the club, the lecherous droolings and raucous ribaldry, the clawing and fondling and general manhandling (of women). Mentally, she discounted all these as lust, not love. She was disgusted with such things and indeed when they went on too long in her story books she penalised them by dropping off to sleep. For her, romance had not yet come. When it did she knew exactly what she would want, modesty not boastfulness, gentleness not goatiness, hand-holding not incontinent passion. At least for the moment that was her definition of romance and love.

Life was therefore quite simple and carefree for her. She was a lollipop-licking bystander, a supremely innocent observer amid the torrid goings-on at Nan-mei-su. She laughed and she cried with her many sisters, she worried when they worried, she rejoiced when they rejoiced. She kept her own brand of innocence. She stayed by the side-lines.

She was the interested spectator in life's comedies and tragedies, had no life of her own, no boyfriend, no desire for one, no problems.

Until Billy came along, Billy the shy kid.

Billy was Uncle Foo's nephew. He came to stay with Uncle Foo to learn cooking from him. His mother, Uncle Foo's sister, wanted him to learn a trade rather than waste his time doing nothing at home, waiting for the War to be over to go back to school. So, with Mama-san's permission, Uncle Foo brought him down from Kuala Lumpur and put him up in his room at Nan-mei-su.

Billy was a painfully awkward and timid boy. Tall, bony and underfed, fair-skinned, with bashful eyes and naturally curly hair, he made a lovable picture. He had soft and delicate, almost girlish, fingers and his voice was equally soft. He was so quiet and shy it took him a month before he said more than just yes and no to questions asked.

When Sleepy came to the Nan-mei-su cook-house one morning, there he was, standing like heaven's answer to a teenage maiden's prayer, with the rays of the morning sun shining brightly on him. A vision out of her dreams.

Sleepy stared at the boy. That morning she reached a milestone in her life. A door closed behind her. One started to open before her.

She dropped the book in her hand. Billy happened to be looking at the ground which was nothing unusual as it was his habit to spend a lot of time studying the ground in detail. So he saw the book even before he saw her. Being well brought up, he automatically bent down and picked it up. He handed it over to her without looking at it or her.

Their hands touched by pure chance. Fleetingly Sleepy felt the feather-like softness of his fingers.

It was the greatest thrill she had ever experienced in

her entire life up to that moment. For days (and nights) after that she would re-live that touch and go into shivers of ecstasy.

"This is Billy, my nephew. He's come to learn cooking from me," Uncle Foo introduced him, omitting to introduce her.

Sleepy quickly corrected the omission.

"Hello Billy, I'm Sim Lee," she said with a giggle that refused to be suppressed, holding out her hand uncertainly. "But everybody calls me Sleepy... you know, because I always fall asleep, when I'm reading a book or something... "

Billy did not take her hand. For he recognised it was a female hand. Instead he quickly put his hands behind his back. But he glanced at her, smiled and looked down. His ears went bright red. He was not used to girls at all, especially girls who were not only pretty but also talked to him. He did not know what to do next. Or what to say.

He did not even know where to put his hands, he brought them back to his sides, he cracked his knuckles, put his hands in his pockets, took them out, placed them back in again. He wished the girl would not look at him so intently. Why, she seemed to be focussing a blazing searchlight on him. He could feel his face burning up from the sheer heat of it.

Uncle Foo saved him. He laughed and said, "Don't just stand there. Come, Billy, we got work to do, lots to learn. No time to stand around and talk to girls!"

This proved to be the case — to Billy's relief. He appreciated being put to lots of manual routines leaving his mind free to wallow in his own thoughts and day-dreams, from whence he derived his simple pleasures. For he was at that teen age which enjoyed life more in the dream than the deed.

To his discomfort but delight, Sleepy was all the time not too far away. Watching him, though not staring directly. He could feel it. And he continued to feel embarrassed, confused and yet increasingly excited.

She tried to draw him into conversation, but he could only smile or reply briefly. And then later he would fervently wish he knew how to speak with ease like other boys without being afraid of stammering like an idiot as he always did before girls.

Sleepy seemed to like to stand close to him. That made him even more self-conscious and clumsy than ever. He would drop things and not know what to say. But all the same he was aware that he still liked it when Sleepy stood so near...

The girls of Nan-mei-su soon noticed that something was happening to their little Sleepy. She spent more time at the mirror. She worried over her few pimples. She asked Sue Ann whether she should do away with her pig-tails and perm her hair.

"Pig-tails make a woman look like a child, don't they?"

Sue Ann smiled and agreed to help Sleepy fix her hair.

She agonised over her complexion. Was her face too shiny?

May laughed and told her not to worry, but she could try powdering her nose a bit, that might help.

"Look who's becoming a real lady?" Lily burst out teasingly. "What's this? All this change? *Alamak!* What's happened to our little baby?"

"Sleepy's in love! Sleepy's in love!" the girls made a song out of it.

Sleepy turned pink, smiled with embarrassment mixed with pleasure, did not know what to say. So she turned and ran to her room.

The girls continued to tease her and the more they did the more it seemed to confirm to her that Billy was for her, fate had brought them together, the whole world recognized that they were made for each other.

"Billy's the one for me. I'm going to marry him!" she told Sue Ann with conviction one day.

But how to reach out to him? He was such a shy boy, so sweet and scared-looking all the time, always blushing, so different from those men who came to Nan-mei-su, swearing, full of macho, loud talk, noisy boots, lustful eyes, wandering hands...

"He's so cute! *Amboi!* (Goodness!) the way his ears turn red every time I start talking to him. And his voice, so soft, so tender! But he's so shy, he talks so little. And his hair, so curly and so romantic, just like Robert Taylor!"

Sleepy opened her heart to Sue Ann whom she trusted more than all the other girls. Sue Ann was a good listener and she always took her seriously, no matter how childish her remarks.

"I wish he would open up, talk to me, tell me about himself... Yet, he's so sweet when he's so shy, I don't want to change that... Oh, Sue Ann, I don't know what I want!"

Sue Ann said nothing. She just held Sleepy's hands and let her chatter on.

"Maybe I should do it. Yes, start off first. Hold his hands, maybe give him a hug, see what happens." The very thought turned her on so much her shoulders shivered up and down with uncontrollable pleasure.

"Maybe once he knows I − er, I care for him, he won't be scared. And maybe he'll say what's in his heart... "

Sue Ann smiled on encouragingly.

"But I don't think I'll like it if he comes on too strong. Men are terrible when they come on too strong, too direct... What the heck! Yes, I don't care! I'll do it! He's a nice boy. It's safe with him. I don't think he'll turn rough. Will he?.. No, not Billy, he's not the type. I hate it when they act like animals. He doesn't look the type. He won't spoil everything by going too far... "

Sue Ann just looked steadily into Sleepy's eyes, continuing to smile and say nothing.

"Thanks, Sue Ann! Wow! It's great talking with you. You've really helped me. Thanks for your advice, I know what to do!"

When Sleepy heard that some of the girls were going to Katong for a day at the beach, she knew this was it, this was her chance to draw Billy out.

"Uncle Foo, can Billy come with us? Can you spare him for a day? He can look after me. Otherwise the girls won't let me join them," Sleepy pleaded, pouting prettily, a look of Madonna-like innocence on her baby face.

"Does Billy want to go? Maybe he doesn't like to?" Uncle Foo asked with a wicked twinkle in his wise old eye.

They looked at Billy. He blushed, caught by surprise. "I... I... " he began and continued blushing.

"He does!" Sleepy quickly answered for him. He nodded meekly, one single shy nod, his eyes closed.

"You're sure?" Uncle Foo checked.

Billy nodded one more time, a little more vigorously.

Sleepy had her old bicycle whose tyres had been retreaded so many times that they just gave up the ghost. She had changed to that new invention, the hard tyre, which gave a bumpy ride and loosened all the nuts and bolts and could even dislodge caps, spectacles, dentures and other accoutrements.

Billy borrowed his uncle's trusty old Raleigh bike.

When Sleepy saw what Lily and Sue Ann had done she gnashed her teeth. She should have thought of that too. What a chance wasted for a romantic ride to the beach! Those clever girls were hitch-hiking with their boyfriends on their bikes, Sue Ann with Beng and Lily with her latest boyfriend.

"Who's the new boy with Lily?" Sleepy asked May.

"Don't know, lah!" May replied peevishly. "So many, and change change all the time only, how to keep up? Anyway, this one don't look like lasting kind!"

The girls were understanding. They left Sleepy and Billy alone. As they swam about together the waves seemed naturally to waft them away from the rest of the group.

Billy was a good swimmer. Actually Sleepy was just as good if not better. But when Billy assumed that he had to show her how, she listened with flattering fascination as a good pupil should.

And lo and behold! Three-quarters safely hidden in the water the shy Billy began to open up. He explained how she should breathe, how to synchronize her movements, how he did his free style. The watery environment, the privacy of the secluded yet wide open sea, and Sleepy's trusting eyes washed away the boy's bashfulness and gave him a burst of boldness which surprised himself.

Mother Nature has indeed endowed the female species with the supreme intelligence of knowing when to be dumb. Sleepy acted her part well and was well rewarded for it.

And Billy not only put aside his timidity but also made good use of the legitimate excuse to touch, hold and stay close as Sleepy played the role of a keen disciple eager to learn from the master.

After lunch, the girls wanted to go for a stroll. Sleepy said she was too tired and preferred to take a nap under the trees. The girls without difficulty persuaded Billy to stay behind with her to keep an eye on their things while they were away.

"Hey, Billy, don't forget, huh? Sure you watch our things, keep your eyes on them, huh?" May said with a naughty look in her eye.

"Not just on Sleepy's figure!" Lily put it more crudely.

Billy's blush returned, but mercifully his suntan camouflaged it.

The girls walked off till they were out of sight. Sleepy took out the straw mat she had brought along. She spread it out. She dropped down on it. She stretched herself out prettily on it.

Billy still stood by her gazing intently out at the interesting distant sea. His bashfulness had come back.

"Sit down, Billy!" she commanded. He sat down, grateful to be so directed.

She closed her eyes and waited, her hands opened out, palms up, hope in her fluttering heart.

Minutes passed. Nothing happened. He was still at it, gazing out intently at the interesting distant sea.

"Lie down, Billy!" she commanded. Gratefully, he lay down beside her, his heart thumping away so loud it must surely be audible even way over there in distant Indonesia.

She waited, eyes closed once more, expectation eating away at her heart. She waited. And waited.

Nothing.

She glanced at him. He was close, very close. But he was gazing out again. This time at the interesting blue sky.

She knew it then. It was up to her.

After a little hesitation she plucked up courage and reached out and touched his hand. At first he just kept still, his hand as usual cold as ice, the hot sun notwithstanding. As she began to caress his fingers, she felt his hand warming up fast.

Then it happened. Suddenly he responded, grabbing her hand tightly, but not knowing where to go from there.

"Billy, you're a nice boy... I like you... A lot..." she tried to start some sweet talk going just as she would like to hear, waiting for the response, the romance she dreamed about, sweet and gentle, honey-talking and hand-holding.

But Billy said nothing.

Suddenly he sat up. Bolt upright as though he could not stand lying down any more, unnaturally stiff and hard, crouching a little as though hiding something. He looked closely at her eyes, looked away quickly, then his eyes travelled down the rest of her body, staring nakedly, returning fleetingly to her eyes, then fleeing them guiltily.

Still he said nothing.

And all this while he held her hand hard. So hard she began to feel a cold numbness coming on, despite the hot sweatiness of his unrelenting grasp.

The whole day just passed like that.

So fast!

It was time to go home. And still Billy had not yet said a single word. But his eyes never left her. Her body.

On the way home, Sleepy thought fast.

Separate bikes were no good.

And once they got back home, the chance would be gone forever. It was now or never. Billy had not yet opened up to talk at all. If he did not do so tonight, would he ever do it later? The magic over, he might revert to his world of silence and unrevealed thoughts. Yes, it must be now.

As they rode past a bicycle repair shop, Sleepy had a brain-wave. She shouted to the others to carry on, she had to stop for repairs at the shop.

"What's wrong?" Sue Ann asked.

Sleepy yelled out the first thing that came to her head:

"Puncture!"

"Puncture?" Sue Ann questioned and nearly added: "With a solid tyre?" But she was understanding and let it go.

Billy of course stayed behind with Sleepy. She left her bike with the shop to oil and tighten up the parts.

"There's no puncture," Billy noted.

"How can puncture? With hard tyre?" the shop-owner sneered at the boy, the word " *Bodoh!*" ("Fool!") forming unspoken on his lips.

Sleepy smiled mischievously. Billy understood — or

perhaps misunderstood.

Straightaway he grabbed Sleepy's hand greedily, even there in full view of the bicycle-shop owner and the rest of mankind. There was now a wild boldness in his eyes, a scary gleam, which she had never seen before. Not on Billy's face.

They rode home on his bike. It was a moonlit night. And on the rickety and wobbly old bike the two rode with aplomb. Like a dashing knight and his damsel on a romantic white steed.

But she could sense that some drastic metamorphosis was coming over him. He was breathing hard, not only from the exercise of pedalling two people along. His two arms tightened like iron pliers possessively around her body.

As they drew near Emerald Hill, he freed one of his hands and put it on her arm, slowly creeping it upwards. And frontwards. She noticed the rise in temperature. His hand was now passionate, eager, hot. Like a groping claw. Like the lecherous hand of that old fellow who got such a scolding from Mama-san long ago. Sleepy pushed away the hand. Unpleasant!

As Billy pedalled up the Hill, his heavy breathing from the dual pressures of psychological and physical stress, crescendoed to a noisy wheeze. Also unpleasant.

"Let me down. Let's walk," she said and jumped off.

They walked up the slope, he pushing the bike unsteadily along with one hand, holding on to her hand with the other.

She felt his overly tight grasp, now more like a manacle, a chain of imprisonment, callous and demanding. The grip so hard that it drained the blood from her veins. Decidedly unpleasant.

She shook loose her hand. With force. The resultant

wobbling of the bike gave her the excuse.

"Better use both hands on the bike!"

They reached the outside of the Emerald Hill house.

He hurriedly set the bike aside. Eager and hardly able to contain himself. He grabbed her. Awkwardly, but strongly. She was caught as she did not expect the sudden move.

She now froze. Frigid. Stiff in his clumsy but demanding embrace.

He tried to kiss her. She turned her face away, totally switched off by him. Insulted. Angry. Mortified at this sudden transformation from idyllic romance to plain sweaty lust. Not able to piece together her plethora of new and old feelings.

"I love you! I love you!" he croaked, his dry throat only managing squeaky notes when the moment called for music or at least manly baritone or strong bass.

She pushed him away. Disgusted. To the depths of her soul, disgusted.

"Why? I thought?..." he was totally shocked by the rejection.

She couldn't answer him. She did not understand it herself.

"I'm tired. Let's just go to bed... "

"Go to bed?" he whispered hoarsely, his eyes lighting up in a sudden new blaze of passionate response, his head bobbing up and down enthusiastically.

"NO!" she screamed out in her annoyance, "I mean go home to our own beds − "

With that she slammed the door on him. And it would be a long while before she opened the door to him again.

"And he was such a nice boy. So shy and so scared, even just to look at anyone... And he could change so quickly! Underneath all that, he's a different man, just an animal like other men! Not someone I'd love at all!"

Sleepy sobbed like a baby as she confided what had happened to Sue Ann.

And that was the end of that unpropitious chicken love affair in the Nan-mei-su kitchen. Billy went back to his old tongue-tied bashfulness, if anything, worse. And Sleepy went back to sleeping with her book.

Time would mature the children and their expectations, but for now love was not for them, only the different private fantasies of their adolescence. And maybe, some day, God willing, they would come together again...

CHAPTER FIVE

The Colonel, the Major
and Mama-san

S ue Ann remembered the time Mama-san had
man trouble, or rather men trouble. She had two
men on her hands at the same time and for most
that's one too many.

The girls of Nan-mei-su had always thought of
Colonel Sato ("Ken" to Mama-san) as the boss-lady's
one and only man. He was already around when they
joined the club. Most of the geisha girls from Japan,
Korea and Taiwan also remembered no boss-lady's
boyfriend other than the kindly old Col. Sato.

The Colonel was a generation older than Mama-san
but nevertheless it was obvious he loved her deeply
although he was utterly restrained in any public
expression of his feelings. Mama-san cared for him too
but with an appropriate reciprocation of self-
inhibition. So they behaved towards each other with
the decorum of a long-married old-fashioned couple.

But Uncle Foo, the old Hainanese cook who had

been with Mama-san from before her Nan-mei-su days and was close to her, remembered another beau. Younger, more attractive and dashing, full of the zest of life compared to the portly, ponderous and phlegmatic Colonel.

"Major Oyama, Teri-something Oyama, that's his name. Mama-san called him Terry," Uncle Foo reminisced to a few of the girls one day. He spoke in his half-Hokkien, half-Hainanese, augmented by Mandarin or Cantonese, where necessary.

"In fact he came here with her. Got her this Nan-mei-su job. Helped her set it up. Got these rows of houses evacuated for her for the club. He was powerful. Like the Colonel, he had something to do with the Kempeitai. Liaison officer or something. Don't know exactly what. And he spent a lot of time with Mama-san too.

"She was very happy with him. She was slim then. And beautiful, more beautiful than now. And in love. Eyes shining. Laughing all the time.

"The Major was a handsome fellow. Like a film-star. A permanent smile on his face. Always cracking jokes. Just like Mama-san in nature. Together they could have lived happily ever after, war or no war.

"But no, that was not to be. He received his orders. Had to go. Had to fly off on that mission to Burma. His plane was shot down. He was reported missing. Must have died, of course. What chance to survive in the jungle? You can imagine the blow to Mama-san! Poor girl! How she cried!

"It was a lucky thing the good Colonel was already posted here. He had come as the Major's replacement. He's a very understanding man, you know. Fatherly, much older than the Major. Plenty of wisdom and sympathy. He knew Mama-san was suffering. And he knew exactly what to do, what to say, when to say it. Mama-san told me later the Colonel was such a great comfort to her. Like a father. She might even have killed herself if he had not come along.

"Soon friendship grew into love. And the Colonel became her boyfriend.

"But Mama-san never forgot the Major. Of course she now accepts it. He's dead and gone. But still she wears the Major's heart. You see that gold heart brooch she always wears. That's the Major's gift to her and she treasures it. She showed it to me one day. Behind it there's a sad inscription: "Love lives beyond death." It's uncanny. As though the Major knew it! What was going to happen to him.

"And you know, everybody knows, the Colonel has proposed to her many times, but she still tells him, wait, not yet."

The story was just too good to keep to themselves. The girls who heard it saw to it that it was widely disseminated. So the whole of Nan-mei-su got the details.

And thus everybody was furnished with the necessary background to appreciate Act Two of the drama that was about to unfold before their very eyes. Right on centre-stage at Nan-mei-su.

It was happy news, but a hesitant, slow-walking, sad-faced Colonel who came with it.

Major Oyama was alive!

Mama-san was enjoying her usual high-calorie lunch, lovingly prepared for her by Uncle Foo. Food had become one of her pleasures in life, a fix she picked up while trying to get over her tragic loss of Terry. As a result she had become plump, which was not good for her personally but a terrific advertisement for the wholesomeness of Nan-mei-su cuisine.

"Terry alive?"

She promptly dropped her bowl of rice, smashing to bits that semi-antique porcelain piece, part of a confiscated Ching Dynasty set. The Colonel winced seeing his gift of love to her so carelessly let go, so easily shattered.

"So fragile," sighed the distracted Colonel.

"*Honto desu-ka?* (It's true?)" Mama-san had only ears for the good news. "Terry's coming back to me? Ken, you're not bluffing, are you?"

"*Hai, honto desu!* He's alive, all right. Nobody knows how he did it. How he survived it. The jungle. And for so long. But he did it, all right. They found him wandering around a village. He was unbalanced. Couldn't remember anything. It took them a while to find out who he was..."

"Poor Terry, my poor Terry! Ken, he's all right now, isn't he? You're sure he's all right? Tell me he's all right!"

"Yes, he's recovered. His memory's come back to him. And they're sending him back here any day now."

"That's wonderful, isn't it!"

"Wonderful," the Colonel echoed glumly.

"I'm not clear what his posting will be. The message didn't say. I don't need an assistant. It's possible they'll give him my post. That means they'll post me out."

"Isn't that simply wonderful?" Mama-san said, her mind still on the main news.

The Colonel frowned, looked at her, understood and forgave her, and sighed, "I hope they don't send me back to that dull Sumatra town."

"And to think we all gave up hope for you, Terry!" Mama-san was still with Terry.

Now suddenly she remembered her cherished heart. She quickly took it out, showed it to the Colonel and fervently repeated the words on the engraving. Aloud, with her eyes closed: "Love lives beyond death."

Oblivious to the Colonel who stood by her. Oblivious to the pain she was causing. People in love are selfish, cruel, insensitive. The Colonel sighed.

Mama-san waited for the letter that the Major must have rushed to write to her.

It never came. Perhaps the mail got lost. That sort of thing was happening more frequently now.

She couldn't wait any more. She flew to Tokyo to see her Terry. She told the girls she would return with him.

Nan-mei-su awaited their return with excitement. It was such a romantic story, and with such a happy-sad ending too. The girls all felt sorry for the Colonel who took it very well although they knew he was hurting inside.

"What to do? That's life, what? Some win, some lose! Anyway he old fellow, can be her father even... " Lily summed up.

"Aw, shurrup!" Sue Ann scolded her. What Lily said was true but nobody liked her for saying it.

The girls saw them as they drove up to the Nan-mei-su main building in the khaki-green military car. Major Oyama got out first. Slim, still handsome and good-looking despite the long months of privation in the green hell of the tropical jungle. An attractive person indeed except for something in his eyes. Sue Ann couldn't put her finger on it but it seemed to her there was a cruel glint of jungle beasts lurking in those cold eyes.

Then Mama-san got out, looking radiant with the shining beauty that comes only from love. She was definitely less plump, obviously slimmed down through sheer determination abetted by that magnificent motivation standing by her side.

The Nan-mei-su girls screamed and rushed out to greet them like teenagers welcoming film-stars.

The Major's lips curved momentarily in a thin smile at them. The girls fell in love with him immediately.

Especially Lily. Her eyes fluttered and flashed out blatantly explicit messages reinforced by sexy squiggles of her ever-expressive body. Naturally she caught his eye and he looked curiously at her interesting convolutions.

Doris cut short the transmission of Lily's flirtation, stepping smartly into his line of vision to ask the Major if he could stay for the "welcome home" dinner for Mama-san.

The Major stayed. The Colonel came along too. He was a good sport. The Major saluted the Colonel smartly. Then they relaxed and chatted as though they were great friends with no sign of their rivalry for the same woman.

Mama-san was the picture of euphoric happiness. She never stopped smiling and she joked and she laughed. The girls had never seen her like this. This was a new Mama-san to them. Radiant, overflowing with the joy of life, stepping light and trim, vivacious as a jumpy teenage girl.

Uncle Foo, peeping out from the kitchen door, smiled with fatherly joy. It was like old times, the happy days before the Major's sudden air-crash.

Except that the Major seemed silent, almost morose, not the uninhibited laughing young man of before. Which was understandable. The jungle experience must have been mind-boggling, would have aged and changed anyone. He talked much less. He watched much more. His eyes roamed from person to person and searched deep into whatever they rested on. Sometimes they narrowed and glinted as though suspicious and questioning. He reminded Uncle Foo of a wary but dangerous tiger, dark pupils flashing from the darkness of his vantage observation point in the bushes, waiting silently for the right moment to pounce.

The Colonel sat there stiffer than usual, smiling politely as the moment demanded but not more than necessary. He exchanged pleasantries with the Major. He looked a few times at Mama-san. Especially when she laughed with abandon and her voice carried such joy, joy he had never been able to evoke from her. No doubt he had been able to give her peace. Peace when her dark despair cried out for help. But never, never joy like this. Joy like what this young Major, even when so morose and sour, could draw out from her.

"Poor Colonel!" Sue Ann whispered to Doris who nodded her head in sad agreement.

"He takes it so well, man. Don't show anything. Sure, he's hurt like crazy inside, must be, what?... He's real samurai, that's what!" May breathed in admiration.

"Can't blame Mama-san," Doris said. "Just look at

them. Major so romantic kind, hero, strong, mysterious. Also Major her first love anyway. And young like her... Poor Colonel!"

Lily joined them. Her thoughts were different from theirs. She let out her private agony in a hoarse whisper:

"Wow! That Major! So sexy, man! *Aiyoh!* so handsome, Sue Ann! See, my goose bumps all over! *Tolong-lah!* (Help!) Can't stand it, just can't stand it!"

The Colonel came a few more times, then he stopped coming to Nan-mei-su. Mama-san was no longer the same old woman, his matronly and reserved Mama-san. This laughing lady was somebody else's — the Major's.

The Major came over but not that often. Which was, you might say, understandable as he had to settle down to work.

He was indeed posted to his old office. And so the Colonel began to hand over duties to him. The Colonel himself was expected to move out to another posting soon. The rumour was that he would be going to the Army HQ. It would not be a bad posting for him as he would still enjoy the relatively good life in *Syonanto*. And the girls were happy he would still be around.

At the office things did not go that smoothly between the Colonel and the Major. Captain Fuji, who worked in the same office and was a friend of the girls, whispered to Sue Ann that sparks were beginning to fly between the two.

The Major dug up a few things which happened in the past and raised queries and even brought them up to the attention of higher authorities. Among them, the question of Ah Lek's escape.

And the Major also started to change the staff around even before the Colonel had gone off. And against the Colonel's advice he asked for the posting in of a notorious Kempeitai hatchet man — an interrogator, a butcher nicknamed "Zo" ("Elephant") who was known for his sadistic torturing of victims.

The Colonel was perturbed. But he was on his way out. And the Major's star was in the ascendant, being the hero of the day. So he knew better than to make waves. He was not in the mood anyway. He was a broken man, a heart-broken man...

Not long after that the Colonel received his expected transfer orders. The girls suspected this must have come as a relief to him. How could he stand around watching his Mama-san and the Major together, the very man who was also giving him so much trouble in his office?

But the surprise was that he was not going to the Army HQ but to a hot action station, the Philippines. The Japanese were being slaughtered there by the thousands, in that bloodiest theatre of the Pacific War.

Captain Fuji leaked out that it was the Colonel himself who had requested the posting. His face was grim and sad when he whispered the disclosure to Sue Ann and May. They all knew what it meant.

"It's his *harakiri*," May spoke it out.

The farewell between the Colonel and Mama-san was a study in tenderness, a tenderness moderated by old world restraint, something Sue Ann would remember the rest of her life.

She happened to be there, out of sight but in full hearing. And unabashedly she eavesdropped in on that very moving moment for two people she had grown to love and respect.

The two were standing just outside one of the club-house windows. Sue Ann was on the inside, hidden by a lace curtain, just happened to be there by coincidence, but transfixed to the spot by the poignancy of the farewell.

"*O-mae*, take care of youself, you understand?" The Colonel being old-fashioned always called her by this Japanese version of "you" used to address women, children, servants and other inferiors. But the way it was spoken it came out gentle as dear, sweet as honey.

"You too, Ken." There were tears in her eyes.

Then suddenly to his embarrassment she threw herself into his arms and sobbed: "Don't go! You don't have to go... I need you."

"*Bakayaro, o-mae!* You have what you want now. Your Oyama has returned to you. From the dead. You two can return to your past happiness. Your young people's happiness. You don't need a foolish old man like me around. Not any more..."

The word *"bakayaro"* meant "fool" but from him it was a term of endearment.

All of a sudden, at this moment of loss, Mama-san seemed to realise the preciousness of what she was about to lose. There was panic in her voice:

"It's not like before. Terry's changed. Not open as before. I'm afraid... I'm not sure..."

"*Bakayaro*, don't you worry, you'll be all right. You two love each other, in the end that's what counts. Both of you have to adjust, but you'll be all right!"

"Don't go, please, Ken! I love you, Ken. Maybe,

maybe... I may even marry you... Give me time... Stay... I don't know what I want. Please help me. Don't go yet... " Mama-san suddenly cried out in desperation.

"*Bakayaro* (this time the tone was sharper, even a little angry), a man cannot change his mind like that! Once decided it's decided. You chose. I accepted. Now I have to go... *Sayonara!*"

"Don't go like that, Ken! We may not meet again in this life!" She trembled with premonition of something bad about to happen.

"*Bakayaro!*" This time gentle with such infinite tenderness, that it reached out and touched the heart of the hidden eavesdropper whose eyes reddened with sympathetic tears.

Then came the finality of his soft but firm "*Sayonara!*" So away the Colonel went to war.

Mama-san and Nan-mei-su waited in fear and suspense.

And in less than a month the news came.

Colonel Kenchiro Sato was to be decorated. Posthumously. He had been killed courageously leading a suicide charge by an entire squad to capture a hill from the enemy. In the best traditions of *Bushido*. The way of the samurai.

It did not matter the hill was lost again the next day.

CHAPTER SIX

The Kempeitai and Sue Ann

It took Sue Ann some time before she got over the mental nightmare of that assault by Beng alias Ang Bin. For a while she felt deformed, a kind of Scarface or Hunchback of Notre Dame. She felt somehow defiled and ravaged, her mind exaggerating wildly the insignificant slice of her ear that Ang Bin had nicked off. A token sliver really. A necessary offering to appease Ang Bin's gods and that paternal ghost to whom an oath had been sworn, relentless and irrevocable on the severed head of a cock.

She fell into the habit of covering her ears with her hair and for a long time in the privacy of the bathroom she would spend hours gazing at the mirror...

In time, with the help of Doris, May, and her other friends, she ended her wake of mourning for her iota of anatomical loss. But the inside scar remained and she still harboured bitterness against Beng. For he was not only mere ravager. He was also deceiver, betrayer of trust, lover-turned-enemy.

Lily explained Beng to Sue Ann:

"Beng, he got *Hantu* (Devil) inside. I ever *kena* (experience) that kind before, what! Last time my friend got. She crazy. Playing with fire! She see *Tangki* (Medium) for *chap-jee-kee* betting, get number from *Hantu*. See and see until *Hantu* go in her! Don't want go away! She talk and act like *Hantu*. Face also like *Hantu*! *Aiyoh!* so scared, I!... Beng like that, man! Got *Hantu* inside. Ang Bin is *Hantu* inside Beng!"

"Don't believe! How can? Where got *Hantu*? Beng only like other people. Drink and drink. Drunk like hell. Become crazy like hell!" May offered her views.

"Sue Ann, what will you do if you see him again?" Sleepy was curious.

"What I do? Beng bluff me, he frighten me like hell, he cut up my face! What I do? What you think?"

Doris tried to moderate her view: "Sue Ann, Sue Ann! Beng crazy then. And he OK just in time. I think, because he love you. And he only cut you so small-small kind. Not whole ear kind! And don't forget he carried you whole way back home! You didn't see. If see, sure feel so sorry for him! Big buffalo crying like big baby and your blood all over him!"

But Sue Ann was implacable.

"He bluff me! Make me love him, pretend pretend love me. And all the time waiting only. Making trap for me. Do this thing to my face... Forgive him? How can? No! Next time I see him, I kill him. Yes, I pray God let me kill him!" Sue Ann's eyes went red.

"Don't, Sue Ann! Beng good man. Maybe he little *gila* (unbalanced). Next time sure all right. You know his troubles? His father, killed by Kempeitai. His mother dead also because that. He told me whole story one day. My heart so sorry for him. He told me don't tell you, don't know why. Poor Beng! So mixed up, but I guarantee you he good man, Sue Ann," Doris continued to plead for him.

"No! No! No!" Sue Ann burst out at her friend. "Don't say any more. Don't want to hear. Just stop. Stop talking about him!"

And with that she closed her ears with her hands.

Then it happened.

"Kempeitai got him. They caught him. They caught Beng!" Doris, eyes wide with anxiety, announced to Sue Ann one night.

Sue Ann was silent for a moment while she savoured the news. "So now they torture him and finish him off for me," she said in a flat voice void of emotion.

"How can you talk like that, Sue Ann?" Doris rebuked her friend.

"Right now Kempeitai question him," Doris continued. "They caught him last night. Beng drunk. Got mixed up in bar fight. Some people in hospital. Japanese soldiers. So they checking if he's gangster. Or anti-Japanese jungle people. Major's assistant telling Mama-san all this — you know, that Lt Kato, her friend from Colonel's time?"

"So he still getting drunk in bar and fighting. Serves him right to get in trouble!" Sue Ann commented.

"Mama-san ask me warn you," Doris frowned but carried on. "Be careful! Major maybe come, take you to Kempeitai HQ. Want you for *saksi* (witness). Mama-san think they know about Ang Bin attacking you.

Mama-san say: be careful. Major's not like Colonel. Not understanding man like Colonel. Funny fellow. Can be very cruel, can be very no feeling kind. Mama-san say she worried for you... "

"If have to point him, have to, what! What to do?"

"Suppose they kill him? You want his blood on your hands, Sue Ann?"

"Maybe, that's my fate, Doris. To kill him."

"Don't talk so crazy kind, can or not? So no heart kind. Not like you, talking like that kind. Beng don't deserve that. Nobody deserve what Kempeitai do to people... Help him, Sue Ann!"

Sue Ann did not reply. She just turned away.

Major Oyama did send for Sue Ann. He waited for her in Mama-san's lounge. He asked Mama-san to leave them alone. He told Sue Ann that the Kempeitai had heard about the assault she had suffered at the hands of a ruffian called Ang Bin who frequented certain bars and was a violent character. The Kempeitai now had someone in custody who could be the same person.

"Come! We go now to Kempeitai HQ. We want you to see if it's the same person. If so, we'll punish him severely for you!"

Sue Ann nodded.

The Major looked pleased. Mama-san had told him the girl might not want to go with him. Yet here she was ready to cooperate without any persuasion.

Now that they were alone and he had a good look at this girl he found her meek acquiescent attitude attractive — and promising. He drew nearer and asked to see the mutilation to her ear. She pushed back her hair and turned her face to reveal the small defect at the base of her ear-lobe. There was hardly any disfigurement. Indeed her face, tilted, with hair pushed back, neck smooth, cheeks absolutely vulnerable and lips full and inviting, made an enchanting picture.

The Major took it all in. He touched and held her face, saying:

"Ah, yes, I see the cut. Poor girl! Don't worry, we punish him most severely. I promise you!"

His hands stayed on her flesh. His touch became a caress.

Suddenly he put his arms around her and tried to kiss her. She was ready for the manoeuvre and at once squirmed out of reach, saying politely, "No, please!"

He pulled her with brute insistence towards himself.

She was saved by a timely knock on the unlocked door. And in sailed Mama-san singing out: "Tea-time!" with her tray of tea and cakes clattering matter-of-factly.

It was so pat.

Sue Ann wondered: Had she been listening in at the thin door all the while?

Poor Mama-san! Was this sort of monkey-business beginning to happen to her? The late Colonel had always been faithful. Never like this Don Juan!

Yes, he was a Romeo all right. Lately there had been lots of whispered stories among the girls. About the Major. The Cantonese girls called him *"Ham Sap"* (literally "salty wet" this meant lecherous, dirty, lustful).

The Major told Mama-san coolly, "I was examining the girl's injury. It's not much. But still the man must be severely punished for attacking her... All right, let's go to HQ now, let's see if it's the same man."

"Are you OK?" Mama-san asked Sue Ann, who just nodded. That confirmation was important to Mama-san. A show-down was not. It would solve nothing, anyway. She would not win.

The three of them went in the Major's car to the Kempeitai HQ in that former YMCA building in Stamford Road.

As Sue Ann stepped into the building she noticed how ominous and gloomy the place had become. In the old days when this was the YMCA there were always cheerful young folks about, who came for recreation — games, socials, talks and good, clean fun. Now there was only grime, bare furniture, unfriendly grilles and sinister ropes and chains.

The moment they entered the dormitories, now converted into cells, they heard the moans and cries.

They passed a bleeding man collapsed on the floor of his cell. No one seemed to bother. Sue Ann stared at him, looked querulously at the Major.

"Oh, he's a Communist!" the Major explained.

"Help me, please help me! I'm innocent," a frail, old man kept on appealing from his cell-bars as he saw them walk by.

"He Communist too?" Sue Ann asked innocently.

The Major just looked at her. She looked blank and naive. He did not answer. And he let it pass.

They reached their destination.

Interrogation was in session. A large person with thick arms was slashing about with a cane split at the ends.

This was the notorious Zo of the Kempeitai.

A collapsed figure lay curled up on the floor, twitching in pain.

Then in a sudden hypnotic spell of horror, Sue Ann's eyes fixed on Zo's arm raised high with stick in hand, the arm brought flailing down in blow after terrible blow! And it was she herself who lay on the floor, helpless and in pain. Each blow delivered a blow on her own body.

She knew why. This was the re-enacting of her own childhood flailings. Her step-mother's merciless thrashings.

"Stop!"

The voice should have been, but was not, hers. She was dumb-struck in her shock, as in her childhood.

It was Mama-san whose voice shouted out in outrage before she could stop herself.

The Major glared at her, his eyes querying: "Stop?" He turned to Sue Ann perhaps expecting to see approbation but instead finding equal repulsion. He turned to Zo and confirmed the order: "Stop!"

They went into the cell, Sue Ann's heart now thumping hard. Was it really Beng?

The man on the floor never looked up. Zo yelled at him and he sat up, his head limp and still hanging down.

The Major went over to him. He grabbed his hair and pulled back his head so that Sue Ann now came face to face with him.

It was Beng.

Not the vile red-faced Ang Bin. Silent, square-jawed Beng. Beng with his pale, no longer handsome face brutally savaged by Zo. His ears puffed up, one of them hanging loose, torn by a cut that brought blood streaming out and dripping all over the cell floor. Sue

Ann felt shame and deep remorse. She had made such a big thing of her own tiny mutilation – what was that now compared to this?

One of Beng's eyes was a mass of red swollen flesh and blood. Sue Ann knew Beng would never see from that eye again.

The other eye opened. The eye recognised her. It looked steadily at her. It made no plea. It waited. As though it knew that he was now in her hands. His sentence of life or death.

"Is this the man? The one who attacked you?" the Major asked.

"No!" Mama-san answered for Sue Ann.

"*Damatte!*" the Major thundered at her to shut up, swinging around as he shouted and slapping her with instant savagery.

"Don't lie to me, I can see how you look at him. You know him!" The Major's sharp eyes allowed no evasion.

"Yes, I know him," Sue Ann confirmed in a small, dry voice.

The Major looked triumphantly at Mama-san. Beng's good eye continued to stare at Sue Ann. No anger. No pleading. No emotion. Resignation.

Mama-san, face bruised and hurt by more than her chastisement, looked downcast.

"You've made a mistake, Major," Sue Ann went on in a voice so collected it surprised even herself.

All her hate for Beng had been purged. The excess of penance inflicted on him was his total absolution. All she wanted now was to save the man.

"What do you mean, mistake?" the Major bristled.

"He's not the man! Look like him but no, he's not him. I know this man. We all know him. Ask any Nan-mei-su girl. He come to Nan-mei-su. He sell us things. He get drunk and noisy like hell sometimes, we know that. But gangster or anti-Japanese fighter? Him? This salesman? Surely, cannot be! Your Kempeitai people make stupid mistake."

"Yes, yes, that's what I wanted to say too, Terry. I recognise him too. He came to us often, buying things for us. Things we can't find ourselves..." Mama-san quickly joined in to support Sue Ann.

The Major was not happy at all. Nobody likes making mistakes. Especially Kempeitai Majors, although they could always bury their mistakes, and in fact did.

But Majors could always take it out on subordinates. He turned to the huge Zo and scolded him savagely in Japanese pointing angrily to Beng's bloodied face. The latter hung down his head and now looked smaller in size.

"Can we take him out with us?" Sue Ann asked boldly.

"No," the Major said. "We have to finish our inquiries first. This man comes from Ipoh. His papers say so. We'll check with his home town. After that's cleared, then he can go."

"Poor fellow! For nothing, get beat up! What you say, I stay and clean him up?" Sue Ann asked.

"Why? What's he to you?"

"He's someone we know, that's why!" Sue Ann's boldness advanced another step.

"OK," the Major acquiesced, unexpectedly humane. Someone had to clean him up anyway.

"Zo!" he called out to the dejected interrogator. The latter lept to rigid attention yelling out *"Hai!"* ("Yes!"). The Major fired instructions at him and got him lumbering off clumsily, bringing water, medical supplies and hot tea. After these had been fetched the Major left with Mama-san escorted by the cell guard and a hunched-up repentant Zo.

"Thank you!" Beng whispered through his thick lips as soon as they were alone. Sue Ann saw that his teeth had been smashed broken.

Sue Ann held his hands. Now she could not hold back her tears.

"Don't cry, Sue Ann. Got no time. That Zo will be back soon. Listen. No chance for me. Won't get out. They won't let me go once they hear from Ipoh. About my attack on the Japanese there. No hope for me... "

"Don't say that − "

"Please! Just listen. They'll beat me again. And torture me. And make me talk. Those Resistance people who helped me escape from Ipoh − they'll get in trouble if they make me talk... Help me. There's only one way for me... "

"No!" Sue Ann was appalled. She realised what Beng was asking.

"Only way. Help me. Please! This is what you do... "

Beng gave her directions to contact a friend in a Chinese medicine shop that very evening for a special prescription. She was then to boil the medicine into a beverage as instructed and bring it to him in a flask the next morning, saying it was something to strengthen him and help his wounds to heal fast.

"It's poison?" Sue Ann said rather than asked.

Beng did not have to answer. "Secret kind. Not many people know. Not easy to check. Will be like heart failure. Quick. And won't taste bad too. Sweet. Nice to drink."

Sue Ann had so much to say, no time to say anything. They stood there looking at each other in wordless communion.

"Good-bye, my love." Tears now formed in his one good eye. "Please believe. I always love you. Had to run. From you, from myself. Never stop loving you... "

"Beng, I can't do it..." Sue Ann almost broke down. A torrent of tears was dammed up inside her. But she was strong. She knew Zo would be coming any time and she had to control herself.

"YOU CAN DO IT," Beng spoke out each word slow and deliberate. He too was in control. And now he added the magic words:

"You love me. You can do it. For me."

Beng's friend knew exactly what to do. He asked no questions, uttered not one emotional word or sound, even managed a matter-of-fact voice to explain how to prepare the death potion.

But at the last minute when he handed the package to Sue Ann, his hands trembled and the rims of his eyes turned red. He knew he was his friend's executioner.

The next morning Sue Ann gained entry to the Kempeitai HQ without difficulty, having obtained a pass from Zo the previous evening.

But the guard at the final grille gate gave her a bit of trouble. He had discovered she was from Nan-mei-su, so he felt entitled to horse around a little, started to touch her here and there.

Sue Ann stiffened, told him plainly:

"You better not be funny. I'm Major Oyama's girl. Major won't be happy if I tell him you stopped me going in."

"Who's stopping you? I only do my duty. Have to check you before you go in..." he growled, frustrated. His lascivious hands ceased their adventurous explorations.

He zeroed in on the flask. He opened it, sniffed the contents, caught the tempting fragrance.

"What's in this flask?"

"Chinese medicinal tea for strength."

"I try some!"

"NO! Not for you. It's very dear."

"OK, you can't take it in then!"

"All right then. Go ahead, try it but don't take too much, please!"

The guard drank a few gulps, then another few more gulps.

"Enough!" Sue Ann said, snatching back the flask.

Beng laughed a hollow laugh when she told him the guard had insisted on drinking some of the potion.

"That's... his funeral!"

They knew they had but a few moments left. Zo would be coming along soon. And they did not know whether that expected report from Ipoh had come.

"Can't stay. Too dangerous for you." Beng was worried for her.

"Never mind me," Sue Ann said. "There's something I must tell you before you... before we part. I know now I always loved you. People say there's only a thin line between love and hate... But now for us there's only love. Nothing but love, Beng!"

They remained silent in each other's arms, unable to find words to say. Words? What good are words anyway?

All too soon they heard the outer grille gates open. And they knew their time was no more. Forever.

"Good-bye, my love," whispered Beng. "Go, once they enter. Don't delay. Don't look back. Need time. For what I have to do. You must not be here... Last night wrote this for you. Read after I have gone. Don't read it before... "

Sue Ann's heart bled as she rose to go. But she knew she had to go fast. The colossus Zo had arrived. And he seemed to have regained his confidence, no longer apologetic, once more arrogant and swaggering, once again the notorious Zo, Kempeitai inquisitor, terror of South East Asia.

Sue Ann left in a flurry and confusion of grief and panic, in not a little way consoled that Beng had the escape potion.

Zo slammed the grille door shut with a bang that quivered down her heavy heart.

That evening the whole of Nan-mei-su knew something had happened. Something extraordinary. Rumours were flying all over the place. About the strange drama in the Kempeitai HQ lock-up. It took a while before the story could be pieced together to make sense. It was Captain Fuji who gave Mama-san the facts as they established them at the Kempeitai HQ.

The Kempeitai had found out that very morning that Beng was wanted in Ipoh for a very serious offence — assaulting some Japanese.

Zo came to Beng's cell armed with that information. He found Beng about to drink some herbal tea his friend had brought in for him. Beng at once offered him a cup. Zo accepted, sadistically keeping up a friendly appearance at the start. They had their drink together like friends.

Then abruptly Zo changed his tone and yelled at Beng, confronting him with the Ipoh incident.

The armed guard who had let Zo in (the same one who had earlier let in Sue Ann) was watching them all this while. Zo had asked him to stay behind. His eyewitness testimony later became very important to explain what happened and how it happened.

He observed that Beng appeared frightened by Zo's sudden hostility. He looked desperate. Suddenly he lashed out with a powerful blow at Zo knocking him back against the wall.

At this point the guard aimed his gun in Beng's direction and opened fire wounding him. Beng fell down on to his knees.

Then to the guard's surprise, Zo also collapsed in a heap on the floor. Alarmed by this, he put down his gun and rushed to Zo's side to check. Surely, Zo could not have been shot by his bullet? He had only fired once and he had definitely hit Beng.

The next thing he knew was that Beng had somehow got hold of his gun and was firing away at Zo and himself. This was also testified to by the other guards, who had rushed in because of the commotion. They gunned down Beng and killed him on the spot.

But Zo, that notorious Kempeitai interrogator, also died in that cell with his last victim. The post mortem later concluded that the unexpected blow from the prisoner apparently gave him a heart attack. The guard lived only long enough to tell his story, for unexpectedly his heart also gave way under anaesthesia while the doctors were removing a bullet from his leg.

That was the story.

So everybody thought. But it was not the whole story. Only one person knew it all. Sue Ann.

The tender good-bye note from Beng completed the story. It told what Beng had planned — and executed:

"Sue Ann, I'm going to kill that Kempeitai murderer, Zo. For my father, and my mother. I'm going to give him a drink of the poison tea. Then I'm going to start a fight so they think we died from violence. I shall attack him suddenly, rush at him with all my strength, and crack his head on the wall. The guard will finish me off with his gun. For your sake they must not suspect poisoning."

Beng's plan worked perfectly.

CHAPTER SEVEN

The Many Loves of Lily

Sue Ann looked disapprovingly at the building that had advanced right up to the Emerald Hill roadside, a post-war addition to the campus of the Singapore Chinese Girls' School. She preferred the huge trees that used to grace that foreground and provide a cool school entrance.

Her disapproving eyes turned to the big-eyed teenage girl who giggled and wiggled past her. Two gangling goons who grinned and guffawed with glee gallivanted with her, one on each side, holding her hands, touching her here and there, encircling her waspy waist...

She reminded Sue Ann of Lily. As Sue Ann started recalling Lily, her mind coursed through a gamut of changing emotions.

Dear Lily, when she was good, she was really good. When she was bad...

Indeed Lily began as the bad girl of Emerald Hill.

Flirtatious, shallow, petulant when crossed, tactless and thoughtless.

And yet behind the facade of frisky frolicking, her close friends could sense a longing for that lasting love which eternally eluded her. Sue Ann felt that Lily nursed a secret melancholia, a sugared-over sadness, only kept at bay by her never-ending peals of carefree laughter dispensed pat from a put-on happy face. Her big eyes when in repose, that is when not winking or fluttering or otherwise seducing, were like those of hurt babies or lost children, and could evoke the deepest maternal instincts.

Thus it was her friends who knew her well enough who could forgive her trespasses. Yes, even Doris, for Doris given time was always magnanimous. Even though Lily had almost betrayed her boyfriend Ah Lek to the Kempeitai.

Indeed it was Doris, who understood Lily best of all. It was she who explained Lily to Sue Ann. She and May knew more about Lily than any of the other girls in Nan-mei-su.

For example, few of the girls knew that Lily came from the old Po Leung Kuk or Girls' Home in Chin Swee Road. The girls in that Home included some orphans, but most of them were teenagers snatched from brothels by people armed with the power. These were the underlings of that mighty functionary whose august name was duly gazetted from time to time by the colonial Government with all pomp and circumstance as "the Protector of Women and Girls" under a dedicated Ordinance of the same title. Despite the awesome nomenclature, this personage was not some Godfather or gangster-chief. Nor was he a super-cop. He was just another obedient civil servant of middling rank with commensurate meddling authority.

Lily was not one of those rescued by the said Protector from the brothels. But mixing with those precocious young things who were, she quickly assimilated their body language skills and became just as adept as any of them in the art of attracting masculine attention.

Lily actually came from a broken home. Her father was a Western-educated Easterner, a WOG or Western Oriental Gentleman, a sad breed in those black-and-white days when "East is East and West is West and never shall the twain meet." Neither fish nor fowl (or as the Chinese would say, neither chicken nor duck) his values teetered between both compass bearings, quite lost and hopelessly bewildered between the two worlds.

So when he fell in love with another woman, he did not just marry her as his second wife (as his Eastern half urged him to do) nor did he consider divorce and a new marriage (as his Western half advocated). For better or for worse, he abandoned wife and child and vanished for good with his floozie — an odium and outrage to all, whether viewed Orientally or Occidentally.

Lily's mother, who had been no angel herself, now moved from man-friend to man-friend, as the spirit (or rather, the flesh) moved her. Soon she too abandoned her little girl with a relative, who thereafter shuttled the child from auntie to auntie (real as well as honorary) till finally, when the last of these relatives finally died, the girl ended up with her tiny bundle of worldly possessions at the door-step of that imposing edifice in Havelock Road — the office of His Mighty

Awesomeness, the aforesaid Protector of Women and Girls.

So little Lily learnt to take love as it came. And went. She learnt the transience of love, she learnt to flit from flower to flower, she learnt to draw what nectar she could wherever she could get it.

And the Po Leung Kuk became her finishing school.

And yet, her forbears did not entirely forsake her. These had included exalted mandarins and magistrates, and latterly municipal clerks and their (more or less) respectable wives. Their genes in her kept her from embracing pure and naked whoredom and she always maintained a modicum of self-respect, no matter how vampish the non-values of her Po Leung Kuk peers had made her.

It was Mama-san who rescued her from the Po Leung Kuk. The *Gunsei-kanbu* (Japanese Military Administration) offered her free choice of any of the girls there for her Nan-mei-su requirements. She chose a few with well-developed physical assets and appropriate attitudes likely to accord and attain maximum satisfaction for all concerned in comfort assignments.

Then her shrewd and discriminating eye took in Lily. She felt only pity for the wide-eyed waif who stood there so vulnerable and innocent, actually pleading with her eyes to be chosen and taken away. She liked her lively disposition and her ready cheerfulness although she did sense even then that the girl could become too hot to handle if ever she got out of control.

What she never bargained for was that one day the girl would become her own rival, the stealer of her own man's affection!

Lily had many loves, starting with simultaneous chicken love affairs — awkward but exciting verbal intercourse, day-dreaming, hand-holding and cheek-pecking and all that sort of fiddle-de-dee.

Her string of boys included almost the entire Emerald Hill male teenage population. And when that supply was exhausted she did not hesitate to welcome such others as happened along:

The mee-seller's boy who went "tick-tock, tick-tock, tick-tick-tock," along Emerald Hill with his bamboo percussor that advertised his itinerant fastfood outlet of noodle delicacies. (His ticks and tocks would crescendo to agitato as they neared the house of the Nan-mei-su girls from whence Lily would emerge to dawdle with him while establishing orders for the girls.)

The young cloth-seller who packed his wares on a tricycle and pushed them from house to house selling them by the yard. (He spent a lot of time rolling out his wares and demonstrating them around Lily's willing body, by design touching her accidentally here and there. However before he could progress further he ran out of stock and had to switch over to black-marketing for his livelihood.)

The *chap-ji-kee* bookie's runner who had a standing licence to pop into any house, the Nan-mei-su girls' included. (He would surreptitiously touch Lily's hands as they exchanged money and betting slips. He stopped coming around when he got promoted to look after a gambling stall at the Great World.)

Lily developed fast. Like a tropical flower in the sun. Soon there came along those who became boyfriends. But few of them stayed long.

Sooner or later Lily or they would change partners,

occasionally with a bit of palpable trauma but progressively less palpable for Lily. For mercifully the law of diminishing returns made each trauma less traumatic for her. She developed this facility, this self-defence mechanism, which made a change-over easy, almost like just discarding an old blouse, and then putting on a new shirt and trying a new tie with a new beau.

The girls at Nan-mei-su enjoyed teasing Lily about her ever-changing boyfriends. It was the classical joke of the club. Most of the time they were light-hearted towards Lily's seemingly endless pursuit and everybody would have a good laugh.

But occasionally one of them would lecture her in all seriousness and scold her when she seemed so completely callous and unconcerned about dropping her poor beau or, worse still, poaching somebody else's.

That was the case with Lily's compulsive flirtation with Mama-san's Major. The girls did not like it at all — what Lily was signalling to the Major and how he was starting to respond.

At first there were only the naughty eye-flashing, hand-touching at casual opportunities, giggling and teasing from Lily whenever the Major was within range. This was Lily's second nature whenever men came within flirting range and particularly if she happened to be about to change partners, which was quite often. So no one paid any real attention. Except Doris (who sensed that something bad could come out of it for all). And the Major (who sensed that something good could come out from it for him).

"Lily, behave yourself, can or not? Stop all that making eyes at Major!" Doris told her off bluntly one evening. Sue Ann supported Doris, though not in so peremptory a tone.

"What making eyes? Where got? I behave usual, what? Anyway, whose business? I ask you!" Lily retorted.

"Just stop it, that's all. He's Mama-san's boyfriend!" Doris was firm.

"Mama-san's so good to us, Lily. Help us so much —" Sue Ann reminded her.

"Help? Huh! What help? I ask her: I join Nan-mei-su geisha? She promise. But she never do. Just postpone and postpone... Now I know, bluff only, man!"

"She's thinking of you. For your own good, Lily. You can't see?" Doris got impatient with the giddy-headed girl. "You think about this. After the War, who marry you? So what future you got? When people know you hostess?"

"What future? Who care what future? Today is here now, why worry about tomorrow? Today, today is enough worry!" Lily summed up her philosophy.

Mama-san looked disappointed as she read the telephone message for her on her coffee-table. Doris, who was going over some accounts with her at her flat, noticed and asked, "From Major?"

"Yes, er... he's not coming over tonight."

"He don't come so much now?"

Mama-san nodded and lowered her head.

"He got other woman?" Doris asked gently.

No answer from Mama-san.

Doris reached out her hand and touched Mama-san's.

Mama-san took the offered hand and held it tight. A comfort house madam has few real friends.

Precious minutes of wordless communion. And then softly the sobbing began.

Doris said nothing. What could she say? Her presence was what her friend needed. When words cannot mean anything, what for to say them?

After a while, Mama-san said:

"Poor old Ken! What a fool I was... "

"Love makes us all fools," Doris said, breaking her own rule about meaningless words.

"Terry's changed so much... You don't know, he was such a wonderful man... He's become so hard inside. It's almost like, like... he's become one of those animals he had to live with in the jungle. He doesn't care for people any more. He's become a very cruel man."

Mama-san was letting it come out. It was good for her, Doris felt, encouraging her on with sympathetic nods and looks. Mama-san carried on:

"You know last week he was here, right where you're sitting, waiting for me. You know what he was doing, waiting for me? He caught a lizard, he pinned it on a cardboard, and he was passing his time cutting off its legs one by one!"

Mama-san broke into louder sobs. Doris felt: "Poor Mama-san." She said: "Poor lizard!"

"I know he's got other girlfriends now. Not one only. Many. They go to his house in Cavenagh Road. He sleeps with them."

"He still come?" Doris asked.

"Off and on, when he feels like it. Maybe only when he can't get any other girl... "

"Why you don't drop him, Mama-san?"

"I don't know... Not so easy... I still hope. He may change. He WILL change. Give him time. He will find all those other girls mean nothing to him... like our comfort girls here. You know, he was so good to me before. We were so close. Surely he'll change back! Yes, he will! I must trust him... It's the War, you know? The War destroys people, all of us!"

Mama-san's fingers caressed the golden heart brooch on her blouse. That old gift of love with its message forgotten by the giver. The gift from the other Major, the one who loved her before she lost him to that green hell which changed him into a jungle animal.

"Love lives beyond death," she quoted. She could not help saying it with a touch of bitterness and sarcasm.

"Love lives beyond death," she repeated, this time slowly and with a desperate search for meaning. She pondered in silence, then at length she said:

"The message for me is to keep on waiting. Till beyond death... " she said more to herself than to Doris.

That was crazy, Doris thought.

"If I am you − " Doris began.

"But you aren't!" Mama-san forestalled what she knew Doris was about to say.

They sat silent together, each with her own opposite thoughts, friends arguing without words.

At length Doris changed the subject, or rather took it off in a different direction:

"That silly girl Lily's flirting with him too − "

"I know," Mama-san said. "But I don't think there's anything serious there. Lily's practically a baby. The Major's got all those experienced Japanese Army girls, quite a handful for him already! Lily is only a passing distraction!"

"What to do with her?"

"Lily? That's easy, isn't it? Just find her another boy-friend," Mama-san came out with her sound advice. "And try and get someone with staying power. Better still why not try and marry her off?"

Doris thought that was a splendid idea. So Operation Marry Off Lily began in earnest.

"We better talk with Lily first," May advised.

"No, better get her good boyfriend, then talk about marry him!" Sue Ann advocated.

May disagreed strongly. So the girls said OK, since she felt so strongly that way, she was voted to talk Lily into it.

Providence provided May with just the right opportunity that night. She and Lily were on duty together at the Nan-mei-su restaurant. It was a Monday night and raining cats and dogs. There was only one diner. He was not even eating much. He was one of those strong, silent, dedicated drinkers who could sit for hours in solitary communion with themselves and their bottle.

So May and Lily could talk.

The rain brought on a depressed mood rare in Lily, but so good for her dizzy soul.

"You know I going out with Major?"

May nodded.

"You know I gone to his house and... sleep there?"

May did not but nodded anyway. There are times when to keep a confession coming it's wiser not to let on whether you are none the wiser.

"After he sleep with me, straightaway he don't care kind. He just up and go. Don't care anything. Chronic like hell!"

May nodded.

"No phone-call from him so many days. So of course I go his house. Not at home, his servant say. But I know he's there. I wait outside. I see him come out with Japanese woman. Don't know what he see in her. Old enough to be my grandmother! I wait till Major's driver drives her off. Then I shout out "Major!" Loud loud kind, don't care. He come out. Just smile and ask me go in. I scold him. I cry. I ask him if he love me. He laugh. Then he is very, very nice to me. So of course I forgive him. And of course we sleep together... But next time again same story. Another Japanese woman. Over and over. What to do, May, what to do?"

This was the cue May was waiting (and nodding) for.

"What to do? I can tell you, Lily. Just don't know you want follow or not! So no use, lah! What for to waste time, talk, talk, only!" She knew Lily was the kind of girl who will say yes when you say she'll say no.

"Who say I won't follow? Just tell me and see. Come on, May, tell me, lah!"

"Maybe you not ready for this."

"Who say? Of course I'm ready. I ready for anything! Not child, you know? Can do what I want."

"Maybe you don't want this."

"Who say? Want what? Don't be like that, lah! Come on! Tell me quick!"

"OK, my advice simple only! Get married. Marry one of your old boyfriends, you got so many, what? Or choose a new one. Get someone your own for life. Then he won't be yours today, somebody else's tomorrow!"

Lily was quiet.

"Think how Major feel! *Terbakar sa-kali!* (All burned up!) That teach him a lesson, sure!"

Lily's big eyes brightened. She was beginning to like the idea. She herself could think of another good reason, but for the moment making Major mad was enough.

Then a look of doubt clouded her eyes.

May jumped in to tackle it straightaway: "I knew it! You can't do it!"

"Who say so?"

"I say so! You look not-sure not-sure kind."

"Sure, I not sure. But because I don't know who to marry. So many of them. How to choose only one?"

May laughed. "Don't worry, silly girl! Just leave it to your big sisters, me and Doris and Sue Ann. You know we your big sisters! Your family, lah! We'll find you A1 husband. Somebody handsome like hell. And plenty money or good salary. Just leave it to us, OK?"

Lily considered for a moment, then nodded her head enthusiastically.

"Yes, OK, OK! I ready. Get me new boyfriend. My old boyfriends all rubbish kind! If not, why I already don't friend them long ago?"

The husband hunt began.

The self-appointed selection committee of three conferred for hours and sifted away dozens of unsuitable men, men who went about their daily lives totally unaware of the cloud that hovered over their heads and passed them over.

Finally the girls settled for three names.

Chan Bong Soo was their first choice. A good man though not a good-looker nor a good-thinker (in fact you might even say, quite the opposite). He came from a well-off Peranakan family in Emerald Hill. He was just a bit retarded but that could be a plus as he seemed likely to remain loving and faithful to his wife through thick and thin. He was a very shy man by nature and his parents, after waiting around patiently for years, had decided to take matters into their own hands. They had openly announced to all and sundry that they were in the market for a suitable daughter-in-law.

Candidate No.2 was Mr Leong, already about fifty, still going strong ("like Johnny Walker" as he liked to say) and supremely sanguine in outlook despite having outlived two wives. He had recently begun to feel once more the old craving for uxorial companionship and spouse services and had confided as much to May's Auntie, who excitedly conveyed the good news to May trusting that May herself might act on it.

The third choice in that order was Leslie, a dark-skinned but handsome Eurasian boy, not so well-off but still financially not too bad, more Lily's type than the other two, namely fun-loving and carefree and only included (as a borderline case) for that reason. He was a piano-player and had recently joined Nan-mei-su on no-work-no-pay terms. He seemed more polite and level-headed compared with most of Lily's friends, having fortuitously impressed the selection committee because he stood up and wished them *"Ohayo gozaimasu!"* ("Good morning!") that very afternoon when they passed by him on their way home to work on the final short-list.

The selection committee reported their findings to Lily. She did not hesitate at all.

"Leslie OK to me. We already met. I like him. You know, he taught me how to dance right way. Quickstep. Foxtrot. Tomorrow he teach me some more. Maybe tango! WOW!"

So in fact nature was taking its course.

All that was required was a modicum of judicious instigation and encouragement for the relationship to conclude with wedding-bells. And this the girls could do easily, what with Lily in the hostel and Leslie coming to Nan-mei-su almost every day and providing his own romantic music as well.

"Les want me go his house tonight. Listen to his old records. What you think?" Lily asked May one night. Normally Lily did not seek anybody's permission for her comings and goings. But this was a special exercise. And she was playing along with all this old-fashioned match-making scenario.

May knew Lily, she knew just how (and even where) the evening would end, no matter what a gentleman Leslie might be. But this could be it, the coup de grace, the prelude to wedding bells!

So May said, "Go! Go! Go!"

The next day when they saw the couple together, the girls could see that Leslie was a goner, all goofy-eyed and jelly-bodied with Lily.

Several weeks later Lily told Doris she was pregnant. "What to do?" she asked with child-like simplicity.

"May as well get married straightaway," Doris advised. "What's there to stop you two?"

And so the happy couple were married. In church, real wedding bells ringing and the church organ playing away the Wedding March.

A marriage made in heaven, a most auspicious conclusion to the life of a girl who had more than her fair share of the seamy side, a "live happily ever after" note of ending if ever there was one.

The girls of Nan-mei-su shed copious tears of joy as they shared these glad thoughts for the one who had made good at long last, the one who would no longer be known as the bad girl of Emerald Hill.

And then the baby was born.

He was fair-skinned and looked distinctly Japanese.

CHAPTER EIGHT

The Matching of May

May's Auntie Mary was one of those persistent maiden aunts who are compulsive match-makers. Having missed the boat herself her one mission in life now was to make sure that her favourite niece did not get left behind.

And now here was this splendid godsend, Mr Leong. As they used to say in her time, the answer to a maiden's prayer.

She was fifty herself (give or take a few miserable years, what does it matter?) and she knew very well that men in their early fifties do not hitch up with women in their early fifties. So she harboured no fanciful illusions about her own chances in the running.

She knew the psychology of men of fifty. At fifty men feel the last heat-up, the declining sun of their afternoon years. And so they cast their eyes around. And presto! They discover one particular group of women, still sitting out the dance of life; those maidens in their early thirties or even late twenties, still good-looking but increasingly aware that time is not on their side. Their fresh morning is going by, noon comes and soon the afternoon, and then perhaps the lonely evening. So egged on by the relentless nagging and pitiless jibes of relatives and friends (and enemies), they reduce their spouse specifications and cast their nets wider. And they discover the men of fifty. And so these noon maidens and afternoon men meet and quietly make their matrimonial way into the sunset.

All this is of course about expectations (and mental strait-jackets) a generation or two ago. Things may have changed. Or perhaps only the numbers.

May was well past her mid-twenties and furthermore dark-complexioned and plain-looking. She was a frank and straight-forward person and mature beyond her years but those qualities count only for love at third or fourth sight, provided a girl gets that far before good men get snapped up by others.

Auntie Mary had been May's self-appointed match-maker for years. It was a thankless task. May was not easily marketable for she lacked the right attitude, she did not care enough.

"Don't lah! Auntie! Can always be like you, what?" she would say. "Like that, what's wrong? You happy, living single life as nurse. Aren't you, Auntie? Independent! Not tied down like slave! What for, husband or children? Big deal!"

"May, how can you say that?" Auntie Mary would be shocked every time. She might be single and happy but the tradition was that she should be neither and she accepted that. Granted that she could not help that any more, it was still her duty to fulfil herself vicariously through her niece.

She had not heard from May since she passed on the news that Mr Leong was available. That silly girl was so slow! Other women would get to know soon. She had to act fast.

She decided she just had to take things into her own hands. May had arranged to come over to her house in East Coast Road the following Monday afternoon when she would be off-duty. The tide would be right and she wanted to swim.

Auntie Mary went to see Leong. She briefed him about May, showed him the girl's photograph which was taken in a studio and carefully touched up to look good. Her sharp eyes noticed that Leong liked the photo.

"Our May quite clever girl, you know. Very well brought up. Kind-hearted. Honest. Obedient girl. Good cook and very neat and tidy kind. Not beauty queen type but face can do. Nah! you can see for yourself from her photo! Not bad, what?"

"No, I don't expect a beauty queen but of course the girl must not be ugly too. Beauty's only skin-deep, as they say."

"Good! Come to my house Monday afternoon. You meet my May there. She coming for a swim. You can swim?"

"I can swim? Come on, lah! You forgot, huh? I'm champion swimmer, man! I don't like to be boaster cock but, you know, I was first in our club free-style last year."

"Good, good! You can teach her swimming. So you have good excuse to go beach with her... Not many people around on Mondays. Plenty of chance for romance! Remember, if you like her, you chase her, you know! She's not the man-chaser type herself. She even say don't mind not get married, that silly girl!"

May was surprised to find Leong at her Auntie Mary's house. She had come over to stay overnight, looking forward to a quiet time by herself swimming and reading and resting by the sea.

At first she was peeved. She knew exactly what was in her Auntie Mary's mind. However Leong seemed an understanding sort of fellow and he did not come on strongly at her. That would have been tiresome.

May decided that she might as well find out more about the man, just in case Lily's first choice, Leslie, got knocked out in the running and her friends had to select a replacement quickly.

"Tell me about yourself!" May asked Leong directly. Auntie Mary was thrilled. Leong was pleasantly surprised. He liked her no-nonsense direct-to-the-point approach.

Leong began a bit diffidently on his resume. As any fifty-year-old can tell you, resumes get longer with age and take more time to recite and can sometimes bore people.

May did not seem bored at all. To Leong's delight, she even asked for paper and pencil and started taking down notes. What a methodical girl! So unlike those giddy-headed pretty young things who were only interested in a good time.

But as May jotted down Leong's curriculum vitae, to his consternation, he saw her shaking her head. What was wrong? Which part did she not like?

Then to his relief and rapture, he heard her

murmur: "Too good! Really too good!" At fifty, it is ecstasy to be so appreciated by a girl almost half your age.

May was of course evaluating him vis-a-vis Lily. But how was Leong to know?

"Hey, May! You real lucky one, you know? Leong, he's champion swimmer one. Can teach you new strokes, man! What about go and try?" Auntie May suggested.

"Good idea! Can we go now?" said May, happy that the day would not be a total loss. Leong smiled, happy at May's obvious happiness.

They had a great day together. Leong liked May's honest-to-goodness directness. May liked Leong's old-fashioned charm, his good manners, and his relaxed free style both in the water and out of it.

Leong did not try any heavy romantic stuff on her at that first meeting. That she also appreciated. He clearly understood women. (He had not grown grey hairs in vain.) She was not to be rushed.

"May I have the pleasure of calling on you again, my dear?" he asked before he left. May blushed. He made her feel like a duchess in a grand mansion receiving a farewell salutation from a royal suitor. She had seen that in a movie or read it somewhere in romantic fiction in her teenage days long, long ago.

Leong saw the blush and seized the moment. He took her hand and with a sweeping bow, bent down, kissed it and was off. A splendid exit which left May, heart a-fluttering and head lighter than it had ever been for a long time.

Back at Nan-mei-su May was glad Lily did not need

a replacement. It was a strangely great relief to her that Lily's romance with Les was going well. So Leong would not be needed as stand-by for Lily.

Doris, Sue Ann and May had arranged to keep a sisterly eye on the two of them to ensure that things went smoothly.

That was why the three girls kept peeping at them.

But Doris was surprised to see a totally new expression on May's face, a look of dreaminess as she watched Lily and Les kissing each other that night.

May looked so dazed and starry-eyed, so unlike the normally down-to-earth May, Doris had to shake her by the shoulders to get her back on terra firma.

"Love is wonderful thing, isn't it, Doris?"

"It sure is," Doris replied, not sure what that was all about.

That night Mama-san invited the girls to her flat. She was having one of her get-togethers which was her way to let the girls enjoy some of the goodies meant for the Japanese.

After dinner, she would always ask the girls to sing for the entertainment of all.

When it came to May's turn she would usually sing one of those booming military songs which were so popular in the Japanese language schools because the tunes were so catchy and the words so easy to learn.

But this time May chose to sing "*Hamabe no uta*" ("The song of the sea-shore"), an old sentimental love song. Perhaps it was because it was unexpected coming from May. Or perhaps there was a magic quality now in her voice, a mandate to sing of love. Her rendition was so gentle and touching, especially in the dim light of Mama-san's balcony, it brought tears to the eyes of the girls.

Doris felt an ache of heart, an old wound of love, remembering her lost Ah Lek.

Sue Ann cried once, and once over again. For her double loss.

Sleepy thought of Billy whom she liked and didn't like, yearned for and yet not, still haunted by a passion she was not yet ready for.

An out-of-this-world mood of soft hysteria possessed them. Everyone remembered something sad and yet beautiful, and the haunting sounds of the age-old song would not let their hearts go without exacting from each one a private tribute of silent or unshed tears.

Mama-san looked at the sea of sad faces around her. By now everybody was singing the repeat verses with May or humming along. Mama-san wept in her own heart, yearning in vain both for the lover she had rejected and the lover now rejecting her.

"Bad news! Bad news!" Auntie Mary said on the phone to May the next day.

A fatal obstacle had surfaced, a stumbling block to Auntie Mary's plans for May. An invincible competitor. Ah Lan, only sister of Leong's rich boss, Mr Tan.

Ah Lan, not a day over thirty-eight, had an urgent problem which cried out for immediate solution. Her sickly fiance of long-standing affiliation (due to his sickliness) had inconsiderately just passed away leaving the poor woman absolutely distraught and inconsolable.

"Where I find husband now? Who want me?" poor Ah Lan wept oceans in abject self-pity.

Her brother put on his thinking cap and reviewed

the situation. It was not hopeless. While there's money, there's hope.

And there right before him was his book-keeper Leong, a gentleman and a good catch for any, although he was fifty plus and twice-widowed with that unfortunate habit of losing his wives. The biggest plus factor was that Leong was his employee and furthermore at an age at which he would find difficulty getting another job.

So Leong was given an offer he could not refuse. Get hitched in or get axed out. Not so much in so many words, but behind the sweet talk the boss made clear his meaning.

That evening May got special permission from Mama-san to take off to see Leong. The poor man was in the dumps. He just sat there glumly holding May's sympathetic hands. Yes, they had reached that stage, i.e. hand-holding.

In due course, had not cruel fate intervened, they would have progressed to hugs and then no doubt on to kisses. But at the moment it looked like those delectable phases of their courtship would never come to pass.

"What the heck!" said May, throwing decorum to the winds and herself into Leong's horrified but nevertheless ready arms.

From the hugging straight on to the kissing. And before more serious progress could be achieved, Auntie Mary discreetly happened along coughing noisily.

"What you do, Leong?" Auntie Mary asked.

"What can I do? If I turn down my boss, I get the sack. Where can I get work?... On the other hand, I can take a chance. Not so easy for him to get another book-keeper? No, maybe he can! There's that assistant of mine, that young Tony. That boy's always ready only! Will take on anything, don't care if he can handle or not!"

After a long session of agonizing in vain, May and Leong went for a walk on the moonlit beach, still wrestling with the problem.

"Why not you get Tony to do it? Marry her!" May suggested.

"Thought of that already, May. But that's impossible, man! He's only twenty something, lah. She's at least ten years older... But Tony himself, he wouldn't mind at all! He's the type, will sell his soul to the devil to succeed, he's that kind!"

"OK then, we face it together. If no job, still no problem, can live on my pay, what?" May ventured.

Leong recoiled in sheer horror, his good old-fashioned soul thoroughly scandalised by the thought of a man living off his wife's earnings. He did not have to speak. His face said it all.

May knew better than to argue with such deep-rooted tenets of life. So she concluded gloomily.

"No way out then? You got to marry that woman!"

May then remembered that premonition of sorrow in love, that strange mood the previous night in Mama-san's flat, when everybody cried or looked like crying as they sang that hauntingly sad song. Now in her heart she sang once more that chorus of age-old sorrow.

Hand in hand, May and Leong walked down their lonely beach. Nowhere to go, no way out, no time left. As they parted in despair, May's tears soaked through his shirt. He felt them first warm, then cold on his chest, then painful right into his heart.

Leong sounded Tony. He was one hundred percent ready to help out. Anything for a friend, he said. Not to mention the prospect of a future partnership in the business as a member of the family.

Leong talked with his boss, Mr Tan.

Mr Tan's reaction was a clear "No!"

"Tony's hard-working and ambitious, but what will people say? Come on, man! Isn't he too young for Ah Lan?" he reasoned with Leong.

"Age does not matter so long as both parties are happy," said Leong, suddenly the epitome of progressive broad-mindedness.

"What's wrong with Ah Lan for you? Is my sister not good enough for you? Are you trying to jilt her?"

"No, No!" Leong hastened to unruffle his boss. "The truth is I already have a girl and I love her."

"Who's she?"

"You don't know her. She works for a Japanese lady who runs an Army operation, a lady with some Kempeitai connection..." No sense in being too specific, Leong felt. Mr Tan would only despise May if she was introduced as a Nan-mei-su employee.

The mention of the Kempeitai connection was a stroke of genius, it made May's job sound more important, Leong thought.

The meeting was a failure. There was no change in the plans. But what Leong did not know was that he had made Mr Tan feel uneasy. The mention of the Kempeitai had made a deeper impact than Leong had intended. It sounded like an indirect threat although of course Leong never intended it as such.

That evening Mr Tan casually mentioned to Ah Lan: "What do you think of Tony as your husband instead of Leong?"

She had seen Tony. The hunk in her brother's office with the handsome face, slim figure, broad shoulders, hairy chest and powerful arms.

"Also can," she said with due demureness and absolute deference to big brother.

Mr Tan pondered for a while. He decided. No change.

"Leong's definitely more suitable. He'll make a better partner in our family business in future."

Ah Lan's premature fantasising went pop!

May waited in hope. Give him enough time. He will come to the right conclusion. He will put love first, even before his job and the shame of living on her earnings should he remain jobless.

But the question was did he love her enough to put love first?....

As the days went by with no word from the suffering Leong, May's friends gave up hope and started advising her to accept the inevitable. But May, while nodding, still nurtured a tiny spark of crazy faith that somehow Leong would choose her.

Meanwhile the Tans were rushing through with the wedding preparations. The marriage was to take place in a church as the Tans were Christians.

Mr Tan even managed to get the famous Reverend Lee for the ceremony.

Rev Lee was a bit of a folk-hero. He was in charge of a rural church when the first wild waves of conquering Japanese soldiers came pouring into the vicinity. The farmers and their families sought refuge in the church building, especially fearful for their wives and daughters. Rev Lee not only let them in but later

stood bravely at the church door denying entry to the
sweaty and bloody soldiers though these were armed
to the teeth when they came a-calling. And somehow
(surely by the grace of God!) he got away with it.

The church service was as usual open to everyone,
so Auntie Mary wondered aloud whether they should
go.

"Why not? I want to go. I want to see. Is he really
going to do it? Marry that woman?" May replied with
a hint of bitterness and mounting despair was evident
in her tone.

"Poor May! Don't feel so bad about it," Auntie Mary
said gently.

"I don't feel bad at all!" May lied, adding defiantly:
"We ask the girls come also. Go with us, we show him,
OK? No hard feelings, man! Also ask Mama-san come.
And Major also, why not?"

Doris, Sue Ann, Sleepy and Lily all agreed to go
with May and her aunt. Mama-san had never seen a
church wedding and said she would join them too.

At first she laughed when the girls mentioned that
May had suggested getting the Major to come along as
well. Then it occurred to her that the idea had some
merit. The romantic setting of a church wedding and
the picture of a couple settling down might give him
the right idea too. One picture is worth a thousand
words as an ancient philosopher said.

So Mama-san asked the Major. His lips curled up
and he made no reply, just went on drinking his Asahi
beer.

"It may be interesting, you know, Terry. The girls
will be there as well. And you know, they even got a
good speaker, a well-known priest, to conduct the
ceremony. Reverend Lee."

"Reverend Lee?" The Major's interest was suddenly kindled. The man was on the Kempeitai watch list.

"Yes, do you know him?"

"I wonder what he says? How he preaches?"

So to everyone's surprise, there at the church next to Mama-san and May sat Major Oyama, large as life. His arrival in his Kempeitai-plate car had caused quite a stir and sent one of the wardens scurrying over to Rev Lee to warn him to go easy on anti-Japanese remarks at the ceremony. It had also created much uneasiness in the church and particularly in Mr Tan who kept on looking back nervously in the Major's direction.

Leong was not around. May's heart soared in hope. Perhaps he would stay away...

But no, here he was, the stupid fellow! Large as life, rushing in at the last minute and getting dirty looks from his brother-in-law-to-be. He looked around the church, saw May, perhaps read even at the distance the question in her eyes, and turned away. But he looked again and again in her direction, each time seeming more agitated.

Mr Tan noticed his nervous looks in that direction. "Why's he looking at that Kempeitai man all the time?" he wondered, getting more and more worried himself.

Before he could ask Leong, he himself was whisked out to make the grand entry into the church with the bride.

The church organ played the Bridal March and in came the bride on the arm of her brother. As she passed May, the latter noted with wicked glee that despite (or because of?) the heavy make-up the bride looked old and even witchy.

As Leong took over the bride's arm, once again he looked at May. May saw wild desperation and the agony of hell in his eyes. Good, a thousand hells to him, he deserves it now that he has taken her arm, now that it's too late. Her eyes grew wet. And she felt Auntie Mary's sympathetic hands close around hers.

The ceremony proceeded straightaway. Rev Lee went on reciting something. May stopped paying attention. She made to get up and leave. Auntie Mary's hand tugged her down.

"Wait!" she said.

Now the pastor had the couple standing before him, probably about to take their marriage vows or exchange rings or kiss or something. May could not stand looking at them. She lowered her eyes.

She heard Rev Lee intoning the usual formula.

Now he was announcing loud and clear if any person knew of any impediment to this marriage let him speak now or forever remain silent.

May looked up suddenly fully alert.

She saw Leong, body twisted around and staring in her direction. Their eyes met. This was it. The last chance. She prayed in her heart for someone, anyone at all, to raise an objection.

Then the miracle happened!

"I'm sorry, I have to say something."

The voice was hoarse but familiar. May looked around the church to discover who had spoken, who was her saviour? She could not find anyone. Was it her imagination? Wishful thinking?

But no! There WAS a minor commotion at the altar.

"I'm sorry."

It was the bridegroom himself who had objected!

Leong was still struggling to explain to Mr Tan. He was pointing hopelessly in the general direction where May sat with Mama-san and the Major.

"It's the reason I told you about... You understand?"

"Yes, I understand," Mr Tan replied without hesitation. He sounded relieved.

"You do?" Leong was stunned.

How could he have known that Mr Tan had been in cold sweat wondering how he could get out of the mess he had created for himself?

Leong's girlfriend obviously had connections. The Kempeitai was literally on her side, otherwise why should their chief come in person and sit pointedly next to her, all the while staring unsmiling at the people at the centre of the church.

Mr Tan knew how dangerous it was to offend the Kempeitai.

And on careful reflection, Ah Lan's problem was really no problem at all. He could get anyone to marry her.

For example, Tony "also can."

CHAPTER NINE

The Last Days of Nan-mei-su

Sue Ann recalled that day when with mixed feelings she heard once more the wail of sirens. Air-raid sirens that warned of bomb attacks. This time it was the B-29 bombers of the Allied Forces as they flew high over *Syonanto*. The tables were turned. It was the Allies bombing the Japanese now. But they only dropped a few bombs, almost perfunctorily as though putting on a show but careful not to damage what they would soon be getting back.

The signs were getting clear. The War WAS coming to an end. The intrepid listeners of short-wave news had been spreading happy rumours that the War was going against the Japanese. They talked about an American bomb that wiped out a whole Japanese city. (It sounded like a science fiction exaggeration.) It would not be long now, they were confident.

The conquerors were beginning to look more and more depressed. Although the Kempeitai still swaggered around, they were less visible, never seen alone, and there was now hesitation and uncertainty in their responses as they vacillated between desperate bravado and prudent tolerance.

A few Union Jacks suddenly appeared on buildings here and there but these were premature and swiftly removed. Later the rate of appearance would outstrip the pace of removal.

The girls at Nan-mei-su noticed that their business was declining. Fewer customers were coming, and those that did were far from a happy lot. Many came just to get drunk and these ended their evenings unconscious or unruly.

Some of the girls started to leave. Some just disappeared without so much as a good-bye. They saw the writing on the wall. Once the Japanese were gone there was no telling what people might do to them. Many local folks all along thought they were prostitutes to the soldiers, drawing no distinction between them and the geishas. Many would even stigmatise them as such just for serving the soldiers as waitresses or whatever. Once the Japanese packed off there was bound to be a witch-hunt for collaborators, failing which any other available scape-goats would do.

Mama-san invited the girls over to her flat. She talked frankly with them. She had become very attached to them.

"Yes. It is true. It's going to be all over soon," she confirmed the news to them that evening. "Japan has lost. Nan-mei-su may go on for just a little while. I have no orders. But it will close. Very soon.

"This is the end. I don't know what's going to happen to my country now..."

Tears flowed down her pale cheeks as she spoke.

Not for herself. For her country, the country she had been raised to love as her life. *Dai Nippon*. Great Japan.

In privacy she had often confessed to Doris and Sue Ann how ashamed she was of the unforgiveable cruelties and excesses committed by her compatriots. But still she loved her country with a blind love — a deeper love than Sue Ann and the other girls could ever understand even if they had a country, not a colony, to love.

But the tears of friends are always infectious whatever they cry for, and the girls wept copiously with her. Their hearts were palpitating with joy and excitement at the long-awaited end of the Japanese Occupation. Yet for the moment there were tears of sympathy to be spared for a good friend.

And they also mourned the passing of a phase in their lives, the end of a passage together, a life at times happy, at times fearful... the dying of a part of themselves too.

Sue Ann remembered that strange evening. They sat in Mama-san's flat after a joyless dinner with her. They knew it was her farewell dinner for them. They knew it was the end of their time together in Nan-mei-su and Emerald Hill. They were not sure they would ever see one another again.

Mama-san talked about her own parents, both good loyal citizens who were brought up to venerate *Tenno-Heika* — their Emperor who was also a god directly descended from the moon goddess *Amaterasu-Omikamisama*. Mama-san spoke of her infancy and her school years, nurtured in a pervasive patriotism that dominated every school subject and every activity. And even when she commenced her working life, everywhere the environment imbued her with the high ideals of *Yamato-Damashii*, the self-sacrificing spirit of old Japan.

"My country is my life."

She said this simply. The depth of her meaning none of her listeners could ever hope to fathom. How could they? They were not Nipponjin. Sue Ann and Doris who were the closest to her sensed the gloom in her words but they too perceived only the edge of that dark abyss that was her bottomless despondency.

But all the girls knew that this was the end of the road. They had become a family. For some Emerald Hill was their only family, but after this no more. Their tears told what their hearts could not find words to say as they hugged Mama-san.

May was not with them. She had left Nan-mei-su after her marriage to Leong, one of the early ones to break off.

As it turned out Leong did not have to live on her earnings. Quite the contrary. He was still employed by Mr Tan and what's more, doing very well having been accorded an overdue promotion by the latter who for some strange reason had become much more friendly and accommodating to Leong ever since that church wedding or rather, non-wedding.

(And in case anyone is interested, Ah Lan did not marry Tony after all. Mr Tan thought better of it. He was not THAT desperate for his sister. Serendipitously he had discovered one Chan Bong Soo, the scion of a well-off Peranakan family in Emerald Hill. He was already in his late forties, a bit dumb and a lot shy, but Ah Lan was no great shakes either. Bong Soo's family were at their wits' end having failed to find someone acceptable to them for him. So it was all up to Ah

Lan, the question was duly put to her, and she sighed and said, "Also can.")

The main topic at Mama-san's dinner was where the girls would be going to.

Doris told the girls she would be staying on as long as Mama-san needed her. Then she would go back to River Valley Road to stay with her mother.

Sue Ann said that she would be staying with May and Leong for a while until she made other arrangements. She planned to search for her missing step-mother who might re-surface now that the Japanese were going. "I promised my father I look after her," she explained to Doris, who just shook her head.

Sleepy announced she would be going back to her Sophia Road home. "Where else to go?" she said, just in case there were offers.

"What about Billy?" someone asked her.

"Don't know! Why ask me? You think I care, *ka?* Why don't you ask other people? I think he's gone back upcountry already. Never even said good-bye to anybody. Good riddance to bad rubbish, I say!"

Lily had come back to Emerald Hill and was at Mama-san's dinner together with the other girls that evening.

She and her baby boy, Les Junior, had finally been deserted by Leslie who had gone back to his mother. To be fair to Leslie, he had tried to make their marriage work. Leslie had been persuaded by his saintly parish priest, Father D'Almeida, to forgive and forget. He did his best. He found forgiving easier. Forgetting was another matter. What with the living evidence before him day in and day out yelling out what sounded to Leslie very much like Nippongo baby-cries. It simply wasn't working. So, abandoned by the man of the house, mother and baby came back to Nan-mei-su for help.

Her friends were willing to let her and Junior stay with them at Emerald Hill. It was against the rules but who cared any more? Not even Doris now. The world was crumbling around them and the rules crumbled too.

But none of the girls had time for Lily's problem with Leslie and her Japanese baby. Their worries for their own future were more than enough problem for them. Where to find time to help Lily solve her problems?

It was left to Mama-san, her own low spirits notwithstanding, to worry and fuss about for a solution to Lily's troubles.

Strangely, the baby seemed to lift her out of her slough of despondency. She tickled the sad-looking baby to cheer him up, got him to laugh, then in consequence smiled her own first smile in a long while. The smiling infant seemed so cute to her it now kindled a wild hope in her breast.

She plucked up courage and put it to the Major. Would he adopt the lovely boy? He was after all his son, although Mama-san did not say so to him in so many words. (Nobody dared to say so openly, not even Lily.) Mama-san pointedly offered to look after the adopted baby for him. If necessary, all her life, putting it even more pointedly. Even as his mother, if the Major wished — making her unabashed proposal now crystal clear.

"Bakayaro!" the Major spat out at her savagely,

calling her a fool. He did not even want to look at the child, beyond his first cursory glance.

He stormed out of the room. He had never ever felt so angry with Mama-san. Why in the world should he be saddled with Lily's silly problem? He had much bigger problems on his mind. And why must Mama-san be such an interfering ass? Mother and baby should be left to their own devices...

Mama-san was disappointed. But she did not give up on the baby. Through her hospital friends she found a Taiwanese couple whose own baby had just been still-born. They were middle-aged and had entertained great hopes for their first and only baby. They were overjoyed with the prospect of having little Junior for their very own.

Lily was persuaded to let the baby go. For Leslie's sake and hers. And most of all for the child's own future, for the couple were good people, really heaven-sent as adoptive parents.

Mama-san then persuaded Lily to go to Father D'Almeida for help to get Leslie to make up with her once more. She was sure the reconciliation would be a success now that there was no longer the baby in the way.

Sue Ann and the girls loved Mama-san for all this, her last act of love as den-mother to a Nan-mei-su girl. Here she was with her entire world disintegrating before her, not to mention her boyfriend so cavalier and callous towards her, yet she was helping Lily solve her problem despite the fact that the girl had contributed to that very problem by sleeping with her man!

Was there any other woman with saintliness to match this brothel madam?

At the end of that last evening together Mama-san had one request.

"Let's sing our national songs together. Yes, whatever our patriotism, whatever we have done or whatever has been done to us, we can love and respect each other and we just give everything to our countries."

She then proceeded to sing the *Kimigayo*. Her voice trembled with a sadness so moving that though this time the girls were only supposed to listen they began to join in as well. Softly. Sadly.

Then it was the girls' turn.

"What to sing?" Lily asked. "We got no national anthem. We got no nation."

"God save the king?" Sleepy asked.

"No!" the girls disagreed.

"*San Min Chu I*, our Chinese national song?" Sue Ann asked.

"No, don't know the song," some of the girls objected.

In the end they decided to sing *Rasa sayang* as their national anthem.

> "*... Lihat nonya jauh*
> *Rasa sayang, sayang, eh!*"

Doris explained the simple meaning of the last words to Mama-san:

> "Look at the girl far away
> Feel love for her, love!"

Mama-san commented: "What a beautiful idea! Thinking of your country, your dream for your country, and loving her as a beautiful girl who is far away!"

She had given a new meaning to the song. With that she too joined in the singing. And now she brought to that common ditty an uncommon depth, a rare quality of poignancy, a yearning for something beautiful but beyond reach..

The city, about to be resurrected as Singapore, was getting restless. Incidents were occurring everywhere. Reports multiplied and magnified them.

Some were reliably reported and remained an inspiration to many for years to come.

For example the confrontation between one Brother Gabriel and a fierce and greedy Japanese officer in the last days of *Syonanto*.

During the Occupation the Brothers of St Gabriel who operated a trade school in Bukit Timah (now better known as Boys' Town) were directed to run their trade school in the old Kota Raja Malay School premises at the end of North Bridge Road. During the last days the school stopped functioning but old Brother Gabriel and a few faithful staff continued to stay on the premises to keep watch over and prevent the school's machinery and equipment from being looted. The looters did not come but one of the Japanese officers who was attached to the school did. He arrived with a truck to cart off the school's belongings, probably to be sold off.

Old Brother Gabriel refused to unlock the workshops for him. He quietly explained that the school needed its equipment to resume classes once the Japanese left.

The Japanese officer yelled at him. But the burly Brother just stood there in front of the workshop door refusing to budge. The squat Japanese officer could not physically push him aside. He fumed with frustration. His eyes bulged out in red-hot anger. Then he made his move. In a show-down which could have gone any direction, he let out a blood-curdling cry and drew out his samurai sword! Brother Gabriel must have been terrified. But he remained where he was apparently unmoved and unmoving. It was a tense moment for all.

People nearby quickly gathered around attracted by the officer's histrionics. They stood there maintaining a respectful distance, merely looking on without comment, their eyes fixed firstly on the blustering Japanese officer, secondly on the outwardly calm Brother Gabriel, but most of all on that central player in the unfolding drama — the samurai sword now out of scabbard and gleaming in the setting sun.

Brother Gabriel turned his keen eyes to the onlookers. Most of them seemed to him to be only curious bystanders but a few were fellow teachers. These looked scared and unsure. No hope of any help from them. But after all they were unarmed and not used to violent action. In his heart, Brother Gabriel sighed, prayed and readied himself for the worst.

The Japanese officer stole a glance at the mob. He also evaluated them. Their eyes looked threatening and potentially inimical to him. Perhaps they were just waiting for him to make his move before they set upon him. He was alone. He had his hired labourers outside but if it came to a fight he did not expect they would lift a finger to save him.

He made his decision. The loot was just not worth

the risk. He thundered away in Japanese, no doubt the choicest Nippongo invectives, but he suddenly kept back his sword and beat a hasty retreat to his empty truck. The crowd recovered from the shock of its sudden victory and started to jeer at the receding vehicle. They surrounded their dazed hero, Brother Gabriel, pumping him triumphantly by the hand.

There were reports that some Japanese were beaten up and there were some reactions – arrests and shots fired in warning. There were the Sikh watchmen who carried on faithfully guarding Japanese warehouses and got beaten up and even killed for their pains. And along South Bridge Road, bands of self-appointed vigilantes began to drag out from the buses people alleged by them to be collaborators. These were soundly bashed up and left for dead. Trial and execution in the streets. Instant justice – and instant injustice.

The girls still at Emerald Hill were getting very frightened indeed. Nan-mei-su had been closed. Most of the girls had left. Only Doris, Sue Ann, Lily and Sleepy remained. They had forced the reluctant Mama-san to join them for her own safety and they were in a dilemma over what they could do for her.

May came, banging urgently on their door, in a fearful state. Pale and shaking with the bad news she brought.

The neighbourhood gangsters were back in town. And in command. Ah Sai, the next-in-command to Ah Lek, was now leading them. And now they had a big following. They had appointed themselves to look for collaborators (and as a side-line, do a bit of looting as well). May had just heard that they had broken into Nan-mei-su and was in the process of looting the place clean. They were also looking for girls but did not find any, which was of course frustrating.

Some of the gangsters were talking about raiding the house at Emerald Hill. They knew that some of the local girls stayed there. They said the girls were collaborators too and should be dealt with.

Leong had gone over to Nan-mei-su at May's urging to check what was happening as the club phone had gone dead. It was he who saw the looting and heard what the gangsters were shouting. He phoned May at once. May tried to phone Emerald Hill but the line was also out of order. So she rushed over to warn the girls. They must get out at once.

"Any news of Ah Lek? Is he back also?" That was Doris's first concern.

"Don't know. Maybe he's on the way. Don't think he's here yet. If not, why Ah Sai leading their gang?"

Even as they were talking, they heard a commotion outside. Then a peremptory banging on their door.

Too late to run! The mob had come.

Sleepy screamed and clung to May. Lily and Sue Ann held on to each other for mutual security.

Doris remained in control. She shouted out loud but calm: "Who are you? What you want?"

"Open the door — open up or we break it down!" came the reply.

Doris considered the situation. The door was not strong. Once the gangsters got violent, they would barge right into the house. Their best hope lay in trying to reason with Ah Sai. After all he was Ah Lek's man.

Doris put on a cool mien and opened the door. The

men poured right in, filling the front hall. The girls fell back to the inner hall doorway.

"Why you come and *kachau* (bother) us? You know we just waitresses. We not comfort girls," Doris spoke up. Her composure discomposed the mob. A momentary silence.

"Don't believe! They all the same!" someone shouted. A few voices immediately yelled out in support.

"Wait!" Doris raised her voice. "Ah Sai! You know us, you know what we are, what we are not. You tell them!"

Ah Sai smiled. He relished the power he held in his hands at that moment, he enjoyed the agony on the faces of the girls, he lingered to savour the palpable suspense of the wait. The restless crowd muttered but waited.

The girls knew their life-or-death balance hung on his next word.

Before he could speak, someone shouted, "Hey! They got a Japanese woman here! They hiding her! Their neighbour just told us!"

There was an immediate uproar. The crowd pushed them aside, rushed in, ran upstairs to search the rooms. They found Mama-san easily. She was not even hiding. They dragged her down to the front hall, threw her down with the five frightened girls.

Ah Sai held up his hands demanding quiet.

"So, you hide Japanese people? What you say now?" Ah Sai's voice condemned them.

What could they say?

"What to do with them?" Ah Sai asked. He need not have bothered. The lascivious eyes of the mob were explicit. In a second the assault on the women, which was what some of the men had come for, would start.

Sue Ann and Lily supported each other and prayed. The other girls and Mama-san clung together.

All hope gone. The end...

Then a miracle!

A sudden thunderous blast broke through the cacophony, magnified by the acoustics of the confined space.

A gun-shot, sounding more like a bomb. Everybody stopped dead in his tracks. Everybody turned to the doorway.

There stood the intruder on the scene. Tall in the handsome jungle green of the *Dalforce* Resistance army, a smoking gun in his hand, his eyes steely and challenging, his tough jaws jutting out like rock, a figure to command respect and compliance from any rabble herd.

"Ah Lek!"

Doris who was down on the floor and could not see, heard the name. A name sweeter than any other. Music to her ears. She rose up from the floor, resurrected, born again, eyes shining bright.

"Thank God!" she heard Sue Ann say and she joined in that thanks.

"Let them go! These women saved me. They saved me from the Kempeitai!" the girls heard Ah Lek shouting to the crowd.

"But they hide that Japanese woman!" someone protested.

"That Japanese woman? That woman? She helped to save me too!" Ah Lek shouted.

The crowd murmured. Obviously he was not all that convincing. But the pistol he brandished was.

"Leave them alone. Get out, all of you! Get out!"

The mob heard him loud and clear. And more persuasive than him, that powerful seconder of his motion, manifestly authoritative in his hand.

They backed off with alacrity. Left Ah Lek to a reunion of rare joy. With his friends of Emerald Hill.

And Doris.

CHAPTER TEN

With a Bang and a Whimper

That mob attack on their Emerald Hill house was the death knell for the home of the Nan-mei-su girls. Who cared or dared to stay there after that?

Wet eyes, hectic hugs, lump-in-the-throat good-byes. It was a hurried and helter-skelter end to the happy Emerald Hill family. The preoccupation, the frenzy now was to get away as far and fast as possible. Before any other groups decided they should pay them a visit.

There was no need to guess what would happen once Ah Lek, or rather his gun, was not around to keep the wolves at bay.

Sue Ann packed up her belongings easily. She did not have much to pack. She was off to stay with May. She looked around for Doris. She already missed that woman's bossing everyone around.

But Doris was no longer the leader. She was now a follower — of her man Ah Lek. She did not know where she would be heading, she did not care, she only smiled happily: "I following him."

"To the ends of the earth," Sue Ann added on her behalf, remembering the last line from some romantic novel.

And indeed they seemed to have gone right there as far as Sue Ann could establish. The two of them disappeared completely after that day. She never saw Doris again. That frantic farewell at Emerald Hill was the last time they were together.

What happened to dear Doris, through the years Sue Ann wondered? Was she mobbed again by vigilantes? Or did she and Ah Lek get into hot soup with his violent and unpredictable gangster friends? Or did Ah Lek take Doris with him and disappear once more into the jungle? This was quite possible as many Resistance fighters became communist insurgents soon after the War...

And little Sleepy, where was she now? At that last farewell, the prospect for her was not exciting, but at least she had a place to go. Even if it was a reluctant return to her past, back to her tribal home in Sophia Road. Physically she was still a tiny teenager but her experiences at Emerald Hill of the last days had already placed her on a fast track to maturity.

"Hope Billy's OK too," Sue Ann said on an impulse as they were saying their good-byes.

"Yes... I hope so too," Sleepy responded in a small voice. "About Billy, Sue Ann, now I think... maybe I was not fair. Maybe I understand him. Girls understand things faster than boys, you know?"

Sue Ann smiled wryly. So, in the end, it comes to this. We all understand love – but always a little too late. Even poor innocent little Sleepy too, with her very chicken affair.

Sue Ann sighed. Another loose end in the Emerald Hill chapter of her life. She had not seen little Sleepy after that tumultous day. She could not trace her at Sophia Road. Where in the world was she now?

Lily's baby had just been handed over to the Taiwanese couple a few days ago. She had wrestled with that familiar situation which seemed to be the recurring bane of her life – the trauma of separation from someone she loved. And now, this last day at Emerald Hill, yet another such separation. Separation from her family of peers who had loved and accepted her as she was...

She had already arranged to go and stay with the nuns while the saintly Father D'Almeida worked on that greatest miracle of all for her – the return of a loved one, the hoped-for reconciliation with her Leslie.

And what of Mama-san? Where was she to go? Where could she go?...

Was there any place left in the world for her?

The girls' minds were in turmoil for her. But strange to say, she herself was now at peace. After the hurly-burly of that mob attack when they had grabbed and dragged her bumping down the staircase of Emerald Hill, after all that pandemonium and panic, she had now emerged strangely composed...

"Don't worry about me. Look after yourselves... I have a place. I've decided. I know what I want to do, where to go, " Mama-san spoke with a serene calmness.

At first she would not say anything more. The girls pressed her and she then revealed she had decided to go and join the Major who was with some other Japanese officers.

They would meet their fate together.

It would not be safe for Mama-san to go out and walk the streets by herself. May who had come to Emerald Hill in an old van borrowed from Leong's boss insisted on taking Mama-san to her destination.

So she and Sue Ann sent her to a big old bungalow house she pointed out to them in Newton Road.

They pressed the door-bell many times before the house door opened an inch or so and someone peeped out at them and then came out hurriedly to unlock the gate for them.

It was Lt Kato, one of the men in the Major's office. He looked terrible. Unshaven, wild-eyed, so unlike the handsome and idealistic young officer who often came to Nan-mei-su, at first with the Colonel then later with the Major.

The girls entered the house with Kato and Mama-san. The Major came to the door. He was obviously moved to see Mama-san.

He did miss her after all, Sue Ann thought.

"I've come to join you," Mama-san said simply.

The Major held her hands with his two trembling hands and looked at her, a hint of tears in his blood-shot eyes. He too was a sight. Untidy hair, a few days' growth of stubble on his face, crumpled uniform, bare feet.

There were about a dozen officers in the house, all equally dishevelled. Sue Ann and May recognized a few of them who were old Nan-mei-su customers, Majors and Captains and Lieutenants all. They stood or sat or lay there in silence, asleep or dazed or in deep thought.

On the tables and floor were scattered the untidy debris of an orgy of drinking — empty bottles, jars glasses, food strewn all over the place. In a corner of the large hall, the girls saw jars of *sake* and other drinks, ready for more drunken drowning of sorrow. More ominously, in another corner stood an arsenal of dynamite, guns, grenades and ammunition, no doubt in readiness for any necessary showdown.

There was one person whom the girls did not expect to see there. This was Abu. Abu was the faithful Malay driver who had served both the Colonel and the Major.

He saw the girls, came up quickly to them and whispered:

"Better *chabok* (go) fast, man! They already like crazy. Drink drink whole night. Some want go out there and die fighting. Like *kamikaze*! Some say *harakiri* better. Don't know what's going to happen. I also *chabok* myself soon... Major and Kato-san, they want to give me things from the house, Chinese chairs and vases. I get them, straightaway I *chabok*, man!"

Mama-san, now looking radiant despite the hopelessness all around her, came back to where the girls were waiting for her.

"Everything's going to be fine with Terry and me now," her eyes were shining as she whispered to Sue Ann.

How ironical that only now, when all was lost, she finds her happiness at last, Sue Ann thought sadly.

The Major now appeared. He approached Sue Ann. He hesitated. He decided. He came nearer. He bowed a deep bow. He said a string of Japanese, of which Sue Ann could only understand the repeated words: "*Sumimasen! Sumimasen!*" ("sorry! sorry!"). Suddenly he broke down, burst into tears, fell on his knees to her, repeating: "*Sumimasen! Sumimasen!*"

Mama-san rushed forward. She knelt down and picked him up gently. She cradled his crying head tenderly in her generous bosom of love. She turned partly to Sue Ann. She said, half to her and half to the Major:

"It's the war. The war makes us bad!"

"No," Sue Ann contradicted her. "Not the war. It's hate which makes us bad!"

Mama-san looked up at her little Sue Ann grown up in wisdom. She smiled and nodded.

"Yes," Mama-san agreed and added, "and it's love which makes us good again!"

And unconsciously her hands went to caress her grimy brooch. She looked up at Sue Ann, saw the girl's hands on her battered cross, and the two shared an understanding that did not need to be spoken.

Kato-san came over. He whispered in Mama-san's ear. She nodded. She told the girls to go quickly. She seemed to be anticipating something about to happen soon. The farewells had been said and said over again. No time for any more now. One hasty last hug and she hustled Sue Ann and May off.

"Pray to your God for us," Mama-san spoke her last words to Sue Ann at the gate.

The girls did not realise it then. That was to be the last time they would see their Mama-san.

It was only after the British had returned and law and order had been restored that Sue Ann and May dared to venture out of hiding from those none-too choosy vigilantes who went about assaulting all and sundry.

They rushed over immediately to check on Mama san at Newton Road.

A shock awaited them.

When they came to the address they could not find any house! All they could see was a mass of rubble and burnt timber beams. The bungalow was flattened to the ground.

"Those Nips blew themselves up in there!" a talkative neighbour came over to chat with them.

Apparently the Japanese officers had a noisy drinking party which disturbed the neighbours. There was loud singing and repeated shouts of *"Tenno-heika banzai!"* ("Long live the Emperor!"). Then late that night there was a thunderous and dragged-out explosion which shook the entire neighbourhood like an earthquake, followed by a fierce blaze from which nobody could have survived.

"They found only their charred remains. Pieces of blown-off bodies. Heads. Arms. Legs. All over the place," their informant was liberal with the gory details, seeming to presume that any local person worthy of his salt should relish them, seeing that the victims were Nips.

"They even found one Nip with a woman in his embrace. Imagine that! Hands joined together tight. And when they pried them apart they found a brooch. Heart-shape. With some Japanese words. Something sentimental. Some romantic rubbish. Still touching though, even for Nips. Something about love.. Love going on beyond death..."

"Love lives beyond death," Sue Ann automatically corrected him in her whirling mind.

"So lots of people are coming here nowadays. To pray, you know?"

"Pray?" Sue Ann asked, intrigued.

"For lucky numbers, you know?" the man explained.

"I also," he admitted sheepishly. "But no luck so far, man! I think they must be unlucky spirits!"

To the consternation of the friendly man, the two girls suddenly burst into tears, hanging on to each other for support.

They wept unashamedly for their beloved Mama-san, Sue Ann and May, as they stood there surveying the wreckage of that explosive mass suicide.

They now understood what Mama-san's decision was as she left Emerald Hill on that last day. But they still could not, never would, understand why there was need for such a drastic sacrifice. Killing herself just because her country had lost the war!

"Mama-san, you stupid!" May said from the anger in her heart addressing her friend's spirit in the ruins. "Crazy only! What for to die like this? Just don't understand you!"

No, how could she? She was not Nipponjin, not brought up in *Nippon-seishin*, Japanese values. No *Tenno Heika* for Emperor, no Moon-goddess *Amaterasu-omikamisama* for ancestor.

"Perhaps, it's for Major's sake. She loved him so much, she had to follow him..." Sue Ann conjectured.

That they could understand.

"We'll never know what happened," May concluded.

But she was wrong.

Abu came to see them to tell them what happened.

He had stayed on at the Newton Road house till the very end. He told the girls the inside story, what took place that evening:

"Abu," Kato-san told the driver. "Tonight we enjoy. Last party. Drink plenty *sake*. Then boom! We explode our dynamite. And we die! For our country."

Abu did not know what to make of it. He was not sure if it was Kato-san or just the *sake* talking. He was intrigued. Also he wanted to finish his authorised looting of the bungalow inventory before he went off.

The Japanese officers wanted Abu to stay. Till the end. They wanted him to be their witness, that they died bravely and for their country *Dai-Nippon*, that they were not slaughtered by others in defeat nor were victims of an accidental explosion.

The Major was to lead the way. With a formal *harakiri*, a ceremonial disembowelling with a special suicide knife. It was expected of him as he was a scion of the samurai and their most senior officer. The rest would follow with the self-immolation by explosion.

That was the way they would go. With a bang, not with a whimper.

They piled up the grenades, ammunition and stacks of dynamite sticks in the centre of the hall. They sat around the sinister mountain like worshippers preparing for sacrifice.

They drank. They sang. They shouted their battle cry: "*Banzai!*"

Watching them, Abu became increasingly alarmed. But at the same time he could not help feeling a strange admiration for these crazy people.

The Japanese were not good, Abu reflected, remembering his many friends slaughtered and tortured by the Japanese. But not all of them were bad either, remembering the old Colonel and Mama-san and others. And the bad ones were not one hundred percent bad too, thinking of some like the Major who had helped many of his friends to get jobs or better rations. It's the war, he concluded. The war makes all of us crazy.

Abu carried on with his dramatic story as Sue Ann and May listened open-mouthed.

It was now midnight. The hour had come. The Major stood up erect. He was now clean and bathed, shaven, well-groomed, dressed in white kimono. The rest staggered to their feet.

He said a few words which Abu could not understand. But he saw how they affected Mama-san who stood next to the Major. Mama-san dropped to her knees and collapsed in sobs. The Major paid no attention to her. He carried on talking. Then he raised both his hands and let out a mighty shout:

"Tenno-heika banzai!" ("Long live the Emperor!")

The officers got up and stood absolutely erect, drunk as they were. Mama-san struggled up to stand with them. They all responded with an equally strong cry. A cry of blind patriotism, a cry of defiance to reality, a desperate cry for victory even if it must come through death, a cry for meaning in what they had done and what they must now do. One for the road. For eternity.

Mama-san now stood tall amongst the men, as samurai as the rest of them and her female voice rang out above theirs, her love for Emperor and Country no less than theirs.

Abu saw her hand moving over to touch the Major's. He turned and looked at her. He held her hands. No unseeming hugging. Then a dignified formal bow, just as formally returned, and the Major swung around on his heels and went into an inner room.

In that room the preparations had been made. For his great moment. *Harakiri!*

The officers outside in the hall and Mama-san waited in dead silence. Abu watched their faces. Immobile. Betraying nothing. Even Mama-san's face was a mask of no expression.

A long, long while passed. There was only silence from the inner room.

What was happening? Abu could not stand the suspense any longer. He went into the room to peep, bracing himself for a gruesome spectacle of scattered entrails. For that was what *harakiri* was all about. Abu was told that the Major would have to slash all the way across his belly with the ceremonial knife, pull out his guts and fall forward.

No such sight met his eyes. The Major was just sitting there as in a trance. There were tears in his eyes.

Abu went up to him, saying the obvious:

"Major, you not dead!"

"I can't do it! Just can't! In the jungle I learnt to survive. I learnt too well. Now I can't take my life! I am a disgrace! A disgrace!" he kept on saying to Abu, grabbing him tightly by the hand.

Abu forcibly released himself from that vice-like grasp. He came out quickly and called Mama-san in. Mama-san was surprised. She listened to the Major patiently. She sat quietly with him for a while.

She then spoke some words to him which were beyond Abu's limited Nippongo. She spoke at length. Softly and tenderly. Then sharply, even grabbing the Major's shoulders and shaking him. Then again on to a softer tone. Finally she had the Major nodding and nodding obediently. She was in control. Abu never knew that chubby lady of Nan-mei-su had such iron in her.

Mama-san then left the Major in the room, coming out with Abu.

Mama-san spoke to the officers. What she said created a bit of stir. Abu deduced that she had told them that the Major had not committed *harakiri*. But as she spoke on she seemed to have explained satisfactorily for the Major.

"She said what?" Abu asked Kato-san. After all if he was to tell the story later he should get the facts correct.

Kato-san translated for him. The Major had agonized over leaving the rest of them to die together. He had realised it was not right of him to go off by himself abandoning them to perform their mass suicide for their country by themselves. Yes, he had the duty to remain with them and lead them right up to their very end. Together. He had therefore decided to lead them in their mass suicide. He personally would throw the grenade into the deadly pile to blast them out of this world to join their ancestors.

Abu did not challenge this heroic version. But he had seen the Major and heard him. Mama-san had indeed created a beautiful picture — and raised the cowardly Major from the slime to the sublime.

The Major now came out, a little less than erect. The officers applauded him. For a moment he seemed surprised. Then he acknowledged their acclamation with a bow. He took his place next to Mama-san. He reached out and took Mama-san's hand. He needed her love and strength. Now more than ever. He did not care what his officers might think.

The officers remained standing. A moment of absolute silence. Even the crickets in the garden sensing the drama stopped chirping.

Then Mama-san started the singing of their national anthem in her beautiful soft voice:

> *"Kimigayo-wa chiyoni yachiyoni*
> *Sazare ishino iwa-o to narite*
> *Kokeno musu made."*

The men joined in with muted voices. With infinite gentleness, with such depth of feeling, tears started welling up in their eyes. And Abu could not help it. He cried too.

They now stood there in silence. The moment for immolation had come. The Major stepped forward with Mama-san to the centre. He bent down. He picked up a grenade. As Abu's sharp eyes watched, he saw Mama-san's hand stealthily pick up one too.

"Better go now!" Kato-san shouted to Abu.

Abu turned and ran out of the open doorway as fast as he could go.

He stopped at the gate where there were sand-bags piled up high. From behind the safety of the bags he peered into the well-lit hall.

He saw the Major and Mama-san standing hand-in-hand. He saw the Major's other hand poised with the grenade held up high. It seemed frozen there now.

For an eternity.

Then he saw Mama-san let go the Major's hand, pull the pin off her grenade, roll it gently towards the centre of the room...

Abu knew instinctively this was it. Trigger point. He threw himself on the ground. So he never saw whether the Major threw his grenade as well.

It was an academic point anyway.

A ear-splitting sequence of blasts sent Abu's body

sprawling and rolling across the field.
    BOOM! BOOM! BOOM! BOOM! BOOM! BOOM!

CHAPTER ELEVEN

Return to Emerald Hill

Sue Ann looked at her watch. Time flies. The real estate agent should be coming along pretty soon.

As she stood in the five-foot-way, the picturesque old wall tiles and antique swing doors on a familiar building captivated her attention and filled her again with nostalgia.

Time really flies. The intervening years from the end of the War up to now have zoomed by so fast!

It felt like only yesterday that she met Jim Johnson. Leong was doing business with him and he introduced the big friendly Australian businessman who was at once fascinated by the petite and friendly Chinese girl. It was a whirlwind courtship.

The post-war mood for hitching up was highly contagious and Sue Ann was vulnerable, having been just emptied of her treasury of friends. Apart from May, but then she had to share her with Leong. So she was just ripe for a proposal of the kind which offered lasting companionship.

Perhaps Leong pushed it a little too in order to get more of his wife back. Three's a crowd, even when it's not worse, a triangle affair.

Jim and Sue Ann married and moved to Sydney. Business boomed for Jim and they became wealthy.

Then May and Leong died together in an auto accident. Sue Ann came to the burial. She left a part of herself buried there with her last Nan-mei-su sister, the only one still in touch with her.

Sue Ann came back to Singapore a few times after that. She came on holiday but she also came to search for her Nan-mei-su friends. And for her step-mother. For after all these were her only "family" roots left.

After more than a decade of happy years together Jim passed away, leaving her a widow with no children and an owner of a small but thriving import business.

Sue Ann again felt utterly alone in the world.

Where had all her Nan-mei-su friends disappeared to? Perhaps they felt more secure with their past safely hidden away. Perhaps some had done well or had husbands in high places now. The Nan-mei-su label would beg too many questions. For up to today there are still folks who choose to misunderstand the role of the girls in Nan-mei-su.

Sue Ann decided to use a private detective agency.

The detectives found Sleepy's house in Sophia Road demolished. Their inquiries revealed that soon after the War Sleepy left home and went upcountry, but nobody knew where.

Of Ma they could find not a single trace. It was as though the earth had swallowed her up. Which might well be the case as she would be very old if alive and was more likely to be dead and buried by now.

The agency scored a success with Lily and Leslie. They found out that the couple had been reconciled and in fact lived together for several years in reasonable harmony. Later Leslie began to take to drinks and then to drugs, but with Lily's support he managed to struggle on bravely and generally stayed on the side of respectability.

Then suddenly it was the story of her life all over again for poor Lily.

Leslie had been trying desperately to hang on to his fading youth and popularity by close mingling with young pop singers and music-players. Finally he deserted Lily this time for keeps, mid-life crisis getting the better of him. One day he just packed his guitar and little else and took off with a young hippie Japanese singer leaving his wife on a note distinctly false even as he tried to rationalise it in his good-bye letter:

"You can sleep with Japanese, so can I!"

Before long the hippie hopped off. And Leslie trapped in an alien country at the nadir of his depression and without the saving support of Lily, jumped or toppled off a Japanese pier and drowned.

Where was Lily now? Her parish priest, Father D'Almeida, knew but he was not talking. Not to private detectives anyway.

So Sue Ann took a trip down to Singapore to see the good Father.

He was busy with some of his parishioners when she came but he recognized her as Lily's friend. He agreed to arrange for her to meet Lily the next afternoon. In the church.

Sue Ann asked about Lily, but Father D'Almeida was not prepared to say anything. There was a strange look in his eyes as he said, "I have to leave it to her. How she'll see you, how much she wants you to know."

When Sue Ann stepped into the church the next day, there was only one person inside. It was a matronly lady in a simple white dress and white veil who was praying at the altar rails. She got up as she heard Sue Ann's footsteps.

She turned around, eyes peering expectantly towards the approaching figure.

At first Sue Ann could not recognize her. She had expected to find a distraught Lily but the person now coming towards her looked so serene and at peace that she just could not be Lily.

"Lily?" Sue Ann was not sure.

"Sue Ann!" Lily replied, quickening her approach and falling into her friend's uncertainly raised arms.

There was so much to talk about they just did not know where to begin. Sue Ann indicated she had heard about Leslie.

After they had talked a while, Sue Ann suggested: "Why not come and live with me in Sydney? I've plenty of room. We can pass our days together."

Lily merely smiled.

"You've other arrangements?"

Lily nodded, eyes all ashine with joy.

"You don't mean? You mean.... you've met someone else?"

"Well, er... yes!"

"You're a fast worker, Lily, you devil! Who's he? Tell me quickly!"

"You don't understand," Lily blushed as she explained. "Don't be shocked when I tell you — "

"Lily, you're Lily! Nothing you do will shock me," Sue Ann smiled. Lily smiled too and continued:

"I'm entering a convent. Applying to become a nun. This new Order is for the poor and abandoned. In Third World countries like India. I'm waiting for my acceptance. For novice training. Praying for it to be OK!"

Sue Ann WAS shocked. Lily a nun?

"I thought you said.... you met someone else?" she said uncertainly.

"Yes, I met someone. Someone who will never fail me. You know, becoming a nun is becoming the bride of Jesus. And that's what I want to be. For the rest of my life. Even if they do not accept me as a nun, there's still place for me. The mission needs servers too."

"Lily, are you sure? You really want this?"

"Sue Ann, I've never been so sure in my life. For the first time, I've found this special someone, someone who will never let me down, never let go of me... Father D'Almeida helped me along but I myself made the choice. Believe me, Sue Ann, I'm happy now, truly happy!"

However there was only one flaw to her happiness and she admitted it to Sue Ann.

"I often think of him. Wonder how he's doing. God grant that one day I may see him once more, my baby, if only to let him know I love him, pray for him!"

Sue Ann's search for her step-mother was a failure.

Except for one remote possibility, the last case before she called off the expensive search.

The agency had been looking into the old folks' homes and found nothing. They even checked those very old ladies who did not know themselves and whom nobody knew either. They were discounted one by one either by the detectives or by Sue Ann who would come and see for herself from time to time.

The detectives started searching the less known homes, ramshackled unregistered places, shabbily run by struggling operators for small groups of unwanted old folks.

One day the detectives trunk-called Sue Ann with some news. They had found an old lady roughly matching the description staying at a small home which was part of a temple.

Sue Ann was dubious, having been disappointed so many times. Nevertheless she flew in as soon as she could get away from her business and went straightaway to the temple.

She was too late.

The old lady had died and had been cremated.

"Do you have a photo of her?" Sue Ann asked the old nun in charge.

"Huh! Where got? Such old people, who takes their photos?"

"Did she leave anything? Anything which might help us to find out about her?"

"Nothing! Some people found her in the streets and brought her here. She had nothing, nothing except her dirty old clothes!"

"Did she say anything about herself? Her family? Who they were? Where she came from?" Sue Ann pressed.

"Her mind was already wandering when those people brought her here."

"She must have said something to somebody? Anything at all?" Sue Ann persisted. The old nun did not answer. She switched her attention to some inmates who came over to ask her something.

Sue Ann took out a generous donation from her purse and held it visibly ready to be presented, waiting for the nun's attention to return to her, which it did.

"Perhaps, one of the inmates here might remember? Did she say anything?"

With a big donation now in her hand, the nun felt obliged to be more helpful. She addressed the question to the first group of old ladies who happened to come by. To her surprise, one of the ladies said:

"She said something. Just before she died."

"Yes?" Sue Ann asked patiently as the old lady remained silent.

"I can't remember ... "

"Try! Try hard! What is it? What did she say?" Sue Ann asked, a little less patient.

"Something about two men fighting. Over her. Or was it over her daughter? It got everyone into trouble... "

Sue Ann's ears pricked up at this. She urged the old lady to try harder to remember, it's very, very important, please! But that only served to confuse the poor old lady all the more. She got completely flustered and could hardly remember anything more.

Sue Ann gave up and was about to go, when suddenly the old lady volunteered:

"She was a bad woman. She said so herself. She said she was bad. Done wrong to people, her daughter too..."

That was all that could be found of Ma, Sue Ann's step-mother. It was inconclusive but Sue Ann stopped her search. She now accepted it. Her Ma was dead.

Poor Ma, missing out on so many of the good things in life, most of all missing out on love...

Sue Ann shook off her reverie. For, here he was, the real estate agent. He parked his humble second-hand Suzuki a respectful distance behind Sue Ann's new BMW and came over. Mr Ramasamy was an efficient-looking man, who ran a one-man business operation but knew the area well.

"Mrs Johnson," he addressed Sue Ann. "I've got to be frank with you. I have another two parties interested in this same house. One local and one foreign. I prefer to sell to a local of course."

"A patriotic young man," thought Sue Ann giving him a mental plus. But she was quickly disabused as the young man continued.

"Foreign buyers are less sure sales. They have to get special approval," he clarified, adding (in order not to encourage any false hope of reduced competition): "but of course nowadays it's easy to get approval."

He suggested waiting for the other two prospective clients as he did not want to disturb the owner-occupant too many times. He did not mention it but he also liked to have would-be purchasers trying to out-bid one another. Sue Ann agreed to wait provided it was not too long.

"Here comes one of them now," he pointed to a Chinese couple getting out of their car nearby.

Sue Ann looked at them. There was something very familiar about the plumpish woman.

No! It could not be? Yes, dear God, yes it was! It was dear, dear Doris! Out of the blue. From the ends of the earth. After all these years. And that definitely was Ah Lek with her. Both as large as life. Larger even, for they had put on substance.

"Doris!"

"Who? Sue Ann? Sue Ann!"

The screams of sheer delight were simultaneous. Hugs. Kisses. Jumping about with abandon. Holding hands tightly and leaping up and down in the street. In their old Emerald Hill.

Ah Lek was as pleased as Punch to see Sue Ann too. Hugs and kisses with him too.

Mr Ramasamy looked on patiently. So the parties know each other. There goes his chance of instigating competitive offers between these two. Never mind, there's still that foreign party. But he wished he had never mentioned that he was foreign.

"Ramasamy," he told himself, "you're too straightforward by nature and you talk too much for your own good!"

Doris and Sue Ann were exchanging personal histories bringing each other up to date.

Ah Lek had done well too. He was now a real estate developer among other things and a big shot in town. He was no longer with the gangs of course. That was given up long, long ago.

Both he and Doris made elaborate arrangements to cover up their war-time history. Now that she was high on the social ladder, it just would not do for people to connect her with Nan-mei-su. On Ah Lek's part, for business reasons it was only prudent his old underworld connections should not be known, nor his past link with those Resistance friends some of whom later became notorious communist terrorists.

"Don't tell me you also want our old house?" Sue Ann asked.

"We're sentimental about it of course. But actually we're thinking of using it as a restaurant. We have a chain of cosy little restaurants... We'll buy in our company's name, not ours. We like to remain anonymous, you know. Did I tell you? We've changed our names. He's Joseph and I'm Mary now..."

Sue Ann told them she too felt sentimental about the house. And it was ideally located for her use as company accommodation for herself or her staff whenever they came over from Australia.

Mr Ramasamy who managed to eavesdrop surreptitiously on this last bit of exchange felt that things might not be so bad after all, there might still be room for competition between the two parties.

As the third buyer had still not shown up and Sue Ann was pointedly looking at her watch again and again, Mr Ramasamy decided to take them in to see the house.

He rang the door-bell.

The door was opened by a teenage girl. Her tired eyes were half-closed and she held a romance paperback in her hands. She looked to both Sue Ann and Doris like a vision from their past.

"Sleepy? It can't be!" Sue Ann burst out aloud.

From the semi-darkness inside there came a loud yelp and out came the real Sleepy, their Sleepy, of course duly aged by time.

The old ladies did their inevitable jig and dance. Once more with amazing energy and feeling, all three hugging, kissing, laughing and screaming, three crazy old ladies prancing about like teenagers right there at the five-foot-way, watched in astonishment by Mr Ramasamy and Sleepy's daughter who had opened the door. (She was less surprised, she always suspected her Mum was a bit bonkers anyway.)

Then from the darker reaches of the inside of the house out came Sleepy's husband — Billy, paunchy, no longer the kid but still recognizable.

Billy was thrilled to see Sleepy's old friends.

"What a coincidence!" he said repeatedly as he joined in the happy hugging.

Sleepy brought her friends up to date on herself. After the War she tried to fit back into her Sophia Road home. She found it hard. They no longer had place for her. Neither in their house, nor in their hearts. She was not wanted. So she decided to go upcountry to look for Billy. Uncle Foo was returning there and she went up with him.

Love blossomed anew between Billy and herself, this time around with maturity.

Sue Ann asked Sleepy why they wanted to sell the house.

"Well, we actually had it for a short while only. Since we came back to Singapore. But it's really too small for us. May here is only our youngest. There's also William, Ken, Doris, Sue Ann and Lily, not counting our dog and three cats. So we've bought a nice bungalow in Holland Road and we're moving soon."

Just then in came the dog, a terrifyingly huge mongrel monster. Standing up on his hind legs he selected the perturbed Mr Ramasamy for his undivided attention.

"What a nice dog! What's his name?" said Mr Ramasamy trying to look unperturbed.

"Down, Major! Down, you naughty boy!" yelled little May.

"Major?" Doris asked. And the three girls from Nan-mei-su burst out laughing. Which confirmed in Mr Ramasamy's mind, these old ladies are really cracko, boy! Wait till I get home, have I a story to tell you, Mrs Ramasamy!

Later when May had taken the dog out, Sleepy disclosed: "We're moving also because of May. She's growing up. And well, she's already dating the neighbour's teenage boy so often. We don't like that at all. They're both so young. She gets so upset over the boy. Over little things. What he does. What he does not do. Anyway, it's crazy! And they're too young... "

The ladies spent so much time talking about their past, poor Mr Ramasamy finally lost his cool. They were not getting down to business at all. He called them to order testily.

They responded but he had a new problem. The owner was no longer interested in the highest price she could get. She only wanted the base price advertised, not a cent more. How then was the matter to be decided? Who should get the house?

"Actually, I have another house here in Emerald Hill as well," said Mr Ramasamy hopefully. "Whoever does not get this can buy that one. It's a lucky house, you know. Belongs to a Peranakan, Mr Chan Bong Soo. He and his wife lived there very happily. Right up to a ripe old age. Both just passed away. Their children want to sell the house." But nobody seemed interested.

"Why don't you two toss for the house?" Ah Lek suggested brightly. They liked the idea. Ah Lek took out a coin. Now at last the matter would be settled, thought Mr Ramasamy.

But before Ah Lek could spin it there was an interruption.

Someone was knocking on the door. Mr Ramasamy who was standing next to the door opened it.

In came a handsome man in his thirties or early forties, looking like a Singapore Chinese and yet not quite. To Sue Ann he resembled some folks she knew before but she just could not place him.

"Ah, Mr Ngoh! Come in," Mr Ramasamy invited him in. "This is my buyer from overseas. He's real keen on this house. You know, his widowed mother only passed on recently. And she told him his real mother used to live here. Right here. In this very house, during the War. So he wants this house. He wants to live here. In her memory. Spiritually close to her. He's been told she's dead, you know. And so this is the closest he can get to her."

"Where do you come from, Mr Ngoh?" Doris asked breathless with wonderment in her voice. But both she and Sue Ann did not need his answer which was exactly as they expected.

The ladies agreed he could have the house.

Then Sue Ann gave him the best news of all:
Lily.

E N D